THE SPHYNX WHO STOLE CHRISTMAS

A BLACK ORCHIDS ENTERPRISE MYSTERY
BOOK 2

M. R. DIMOND

Cover Design by Mariah Sinclair www.mariahsinclair.com

ISBN paperback 978-1-956204-00-1

ISBN large print 978-1-956204-04-9

ISBN ebook 978-1-956204-05-6

 Created with Vellum

CHAPTER 1

"Happy New Year! Happy New Year!" we caroled in full voice. It was still a week before Christmas, but an ABBA tribute band has to sing ABBA songs. They didn't make a Christmas album, but Sweden still broadcasts the old video of their New Year's song, with them singing around an old-fashioned piano, like we were doing now.

The audience burst into applause and cheers before I finished the noodley bit at the end—a contrast to the last time MultiABBA sang this song in this place. Then we were trying to distract our guests as the Ly family gave first aid to a poison victim on the other side of the room. We gave up when the paramedics arrived, sirens blaring.

Be glad you weren't there.

But a year makes a difference. Last year, as she made her retirement exit, Johnny's grandmother, Mrs. Ly, introduced us to Beauchamp, Texas, as her grandson and his college friends. Our umbrella company, Black Orchid Enterprises, covered legal, financial, and feline veterinary services, now including an overflow cat shelter. Johnny is both Assistant Animal Control Officer and Assistant Justice of the Peace. The attitude on all sides was, "Who are these people anyway?" As the year progressed,

Beauchamp settled into "Oh, them," and we learned to recognize the signs of friendly natives versus those inclined to blow our heads off.

On the third Saturday of December, Beauchamp (pronounced Beecham) comes to historic Gregg House for the lavish promise of free food and gifts. Beauchamp wants to continue this fifty-year tradition, and most have the manners not to cause a ruckus while they eat our food.

They're even willing to clap for our music (which you can hear from our playlist at the back of the book). We took our bows and glided through the compliments back to our regular party duties. Chantal Gaumont (Agnetha, soprano), long blonde hair of her wig flying, returned to the kitchen to ride herd on our staff of party helpers. We couldn't put on this shindig without our twenty-odd Christmas elves, also known as our younger siblings and cousins, those of an age to think all parties were fun and glad for any addition to their finances. Because Gregg House serves as a shelter during community evacuations, we had enough cots to put them up for a few days in the third-floor attic.

Dianne Cortez (Anni-Frid, alto) headed to the back door to welcome guests, and Johnny Ly (Bjorn, tenor) lined up people to parade through his cat clinic and Beauchamp's overflow shelter. His brow furrowed as he glanced at his sister, Sophie Thi. So I, JD Thompson (Benny, bass-baritone, keyboards), instead of traversing the long gallery hall to greet people at the front door, approached his sister as she danced around and handed out candy canes while chanting, "And a Merry Effing Christmas to you." To be fair, she said it only to adults, mostly men, who looked like they might appreciate it.

Last year Sophie Thi was hurt that she wasn't asked to be a party elf, though her family relationships then were fraught at best. Surprised but willing, Johnny hired her this year, described the uniform (Christmas colors and a Santa hat), and listed the words she couldn't say.

Her dark green tunic met the requirements. It might be scooped too low for a family party, but many strands of blinking Christmas lights around her neck covered and distracted from any impropriety. The Christmas hat perched on one side of her head and the rest of her hair snatched into a ponytail on the opposite side did look odd, but memorable. The tights with one red-striped leg and one green made her look like an Asian Christmas-y Pippi Longstocking. A Vietnamese grandfather makes most people think Johnny is "vaguely Asian," but his sister's makeup emphasized those features to the stereotypical limits, giving her an animé appearance.

No doubt she was making a statement, but I wasn't about to ask her about it. I did murmur that we should include "effing" on the forbidden word list.

She made a face and trotted toward her grandmother's red velvet throne chair. She spun in the opposite direction and added a few dance steps to avoid three middle-aged bros with the same goal. She wrinkled her nose, like they stunk. I'm not sure how she could tell over all the holiday house aromas.

Chantal brushed beside me with her arms full of food—something curried by the smell, an interesting combination with the sugary scents that smothered the nasal passages. Amazingly, she found places for everything on the not-at-all empty buffet tables. Ignoring people staring at her long blonde tresses over her Mississippi River-brown skin, she commented to me, "I'm glad Dianne and I talked to Sophie Thi about her outfit. We told her she was representing Black Orchid Enterprises today and how Beauchamp isn't as cool as Austin. She redid the outfit on the spot! Doesn't it look better?"

My eyes widened as I tried to imagine Sophie Thi's earlier costume. I hadn't seen it; Johnny and I were almost late for our own party. (We sure heard about that from Dianne.) But there's no scheduling when people die, and the Assistant Justice of the Peace—Johnny—has to go declare them dead and decide whether their death needs investigating.

He drags me along in case law enforcement doesn't agree with his findings or request for more investigation. He wants to be dead (excuse the pun) certain before he declares someone deceased of natural causes, and, while we get along okay with the Beauchamp police, the Alvarez County Sheriff's Office hates him for what he does to their budget in the pursuit of justice.

This was one of those mornings, with the sheriff sure that fifty-eight-year-old women drop dead of natural causes all the time, despite the family's wailing that Mummy was in perfect health. To my surprise, Johnny brought the scene to a close sooner than normal.

"My grandmother was asking me this morning what I'd like for Christmas. I'll tell her I'd like an initial workup by a medical examiner for this person. I'll order it."

That left the sheriff bereft of speech, but the family loud and grateful. On the way home, Grandmother Ly and the medical examiner having been notified, I said, "I'm not sure your grandmother understands the Christmas spirit."

"No reason she should. She's Jewish," Johnny replied as he pulled up to Gregg House for the biggest Christmas party in three counties, a tradition established by a Jewish woman and her Vietnamese Buddhist husband.

She had several goals. To stop people from ringing her doorbell all year, she wanted to offer the community a chance to see the inside of the historic Victorian mansion she had bought with her inheritance. As the school district nurse, she knew which local families needed help the most, and she used the party to distribute holiday charity. Most of all, we suspected, she wanted to give her immigrant husband, who came to Texas with her after her tour as a nurse in Vietnam, the kind of Christmas he saw on television.

Though she moved into an assisted living facility in Austin last year, her husband having died a short while before, she attended the open house to see her old friends. I nodded to her as I passed her court, but she was busy with Mayor Lorenz, who handed her a check with a flourish.

After the mayor came two of the middle-aged guys I'd seen earlier; the third hung back with his hands in his pocket. I met him earlier, when Leigh Brandon, our neighbor across the street, arrived with her adult children and their families. He was a son-in-law. The widow of an oil baron, Miss Leigh gave a sizable donation too, but she brought the check over yesterday instead of making a show.

Since we Black Orchids were still struggling to establish ourselves as cat vet, accountant, and attorney in a Central Texas town of 7200, I was glad the entire Ly family looked on this occasion as their major charitable activity, in addition to the Beauchamp residents now bringing tribute to Mrs. Ly.

Upstairs our resident house kittens howled, led by Dianne's flame point Siamese. I'm not sure whether they were commenting on our performance or protesting their imprisonment in cat condos in Dianne's bedroom, but Mrs. Ly cast an amused glance towards the stairs as Dianne's brother led yet another house tour to see the second floor.

The thundering on the stairs drowned out the cats, and before it died away, my grandmother, my first piano teacher, reclaimed the piano to twinkle out soothing carols.

I inhaled to the ends of my socks as I made my twisted way through our guests. Underlying all scents was the evergreen aroma from the greenery attached to every surface possible and the enormous Christmas tree extending into the stratosphere of the cathedral ceiling. I passed tables piled high with holiday treats, food we bought from every restaurant and food truck in town (so as not to play favorites), food Johnny spent the last week cooking (because he likes it and that's how he gives Christmas gifts, by making our childhood comfort treats), and food that guests brought. (I have no idea why, unless it's the Southern dictum that you can't cross anyone's threshold without an offering.) The spread offered a cheery multicultural mélange of sights and scents, both savory and sweet.

To be honest, I was sick of the sweets by the time we welcomed the first guests. Their smells—the sweets, not the guests—stuck at the back of my throat as a ghost of the taste brought on by what began as an aroma and ended as a stink. Not only did Johnny make all the holiday treats of everybody's traditions, but every morning he whipped up a batch of new icing to use in gingerbread house construction.

We added two new features this year. One was a holiday concert, featuring Austin musicians, Beauchamp area choirs, and (naturally) MultiABBA, the sort of event my grandmother used to sponsor in her earlier years in Houston, as a way to provide classical musicians with some income and fame. Liking the idea, Mrs. Ly and her do-gooder friends pitched in, and Beauchamp would return to Gregg House on Monday night to be serenaded.

The Beauchamp Gingerbread House Display was the fault of Darryl Swann, the Black Orchid Enterprises' intern. I don't know whether to say "nightmare" or "inspiration." You never know with Darryl's ideas. Sadly, no one's ever going to forget the Passover-Easter display earlier this year.

Even though he advertised around town in all possible media, we spent the week slapping together houses in case no one else brought one on Friday night. I didn't much like the smell of gingerbread anymore either.

But Darryl can walk into a business and start talking about his great idea, and in five minutes, everybody within earshot wants to take part. That's how he financed and built his previous holiday displays, with donations and labor from the lumber company, hardware store, craft store, and other businesses whose names appear on his "Courtesy Of" signs in the front yard.

The town was thrilled to join in. Rows of tables ran from the front door to the back, half the length of a football field. Local businesses, clubs, associations, and individuals vied with each other in cookie architecture to produce a spectacular Candyland metropolis. Most houses would return to their builders for the rest of the holiday season, except for those that would create holiday cheer at Beauchamp's public places like the library, senior center, and town hall. A sharp, sweet gingerbread tang wafted over the scent of Christmas greenery adorning every surface that wasn't covered in gingerbread houses or food, including the floor, high arched ceiling, and windows.

As I walked past the last table of houses, the credit union manager pushed parts of his display back into place after admirers poked at the chambers to see if the gold was real. Maybe the backrooms of a credit union do look like Gringotts Wizarding Bank in *Harry Potter*. The local bank's concoction was a squat, flat-roofed edifice like their real-life building, but with a gingerbread dragon on top, sleeping on its horde. Beauchamp Barbecue stood between them, with meat and smoker rendered in cookie dough. Even the Catholic Church had an entry of medieval-ish architecture with hard-candy stained-glass windows. The Baptist Church didn't even try to compete with that. They made a model of one of their disaster kitchens on wheels, a gingerbread trailer, its silver finish rendered by shimmering cake-decorating beads.

A tired-looking, middle-aged red-haired guy explained the architectural points of the cathedral to some kids who wanted to see if the doors opened. I gave him a doubtful look as I shook his hand. As far as I knew, he wasn't Catholic.

He introduced himself as the new minister of the Beauchamp First Baptist Church. "Father Emilio had to say five o'clock Mass. I told him I'd guard the cathedral; he guarded my trailer while I was finishing the Nativity Pageant rehearsal this morning. I was hoping to go over my sermon again this afternoon; I didn't realize I'd have to stand guard this long." He frowned as he looked out over the guests—no one in particular, I thought, because the first one in his line of sight was our elderly neighbor, Leigh Brandon, and her grown daughter, Claire, both nice ladies. I don't say that just because they're my clients. I avoid the elder daughter, Melanie, as much as I can.

"You shouldn't have to. Parents just turn their kids loose at this event." I called to Sophie Thi, doing another dance step around the same trio of dudes.

"And a Merry *Merry* Christmas to you," she told Pastor Nathan as she flourished a candy cane. She gave me a pointed look to make sure I noticed her reformation.

He gave the candy cane back to her with an alarmed smile, as seemed to be the usual response to Sophie Thi.

With a nod of acknowledgement to her sacrifice and improvement, I asked, "Could you protect this table of houses so Pastor Nathan can go home?"

"I can." She crouched into a warrior pose as she pulled the candy cane above and behind her as a sword. She'd make a great seasonal manga comic cover. She shouted to a group of ten-year-old boys approaching the table. "Merry Christmas! Have you visited the Christmas tree to get your gift?"

"I'm Jewish," challenged the tall one.

"Me too," she shot back. She shoved her hand into her elf apron and came out with a handful of gold-foil-wrapped coins and a plastic top. "Happy Hanukkah. Have some Hanukkah gelt. And a dreidl. You still get a present, though."

"I get eight," the boy insisted.

"Nice try. Ask your parents for the rest of them. I hope they're all socks and winter gloves." She waved her arms to shoo the boys down the gallery to the Cortez sisters at the Christmas tree.

Pastor Nathan managed a thread of a smile for her. "Thank you. I see that you have everything under control."

As I followed him to the front door, a sharp citrus aroma joined the nasal feast. Yesterday Pittman & Davis' biggest box of fruit from the Rio Grande Valley arrived, a guilt-gift from my father in place of his presence. I was touched; he sent the biggest combination available, the one he sent to his best clients. Party planner and chief decorator Chantal was less touched; she'd already adorned every available surface. She piled the open boxes, bohemian style, by the door to greet people with the aroma of Texas oranges and pink grapefruit.

Officer Alejandro Quintanilla-Villanueva stood guard over the last (or first, if you came in the front door) gingerbread offering, a dungeon made by the Beauchamp Police Department. I shook his hand.

"Where's Cupcake?" I asked, referring to his constant canine companion, almost a police dog—when she feels like it.

"On the back porch," he replied, with a stern eye on the grammar school kids examining the torture chamber. "I didn't want her destroying any of the displays, and one wag of her tail would do it."

His radio crackled, and he muttered some cop-speak into it. Unintelligible squawks answered him. As he put it away, he asked, "Where's Johnny?"

"Doing a tour of the cat clinic and shelter, last I knew." I raised a questioning eyebrow.

"I might need him, but I can't wait. Could you keep an eye on this?" He gestured to his gingerbread dungeon.

"Sure. I'll give Johnny a heads-up." I hoped my cooperation would induce him to confide in me, but he just nodded and headed for the back door. There was only one reason Officer Al would need Johnny, and it wasn't for Cupcake's shots.

A girl from the group around the dungeon stopped him. "Do you have any of this stuff at the jail, like the rack? Or thumbscrews?"

"You don't want to find out, do you?" Officer Al looked as forbidding as he knew how. Just over a year out of police academy, he's still working on that.

I took up a welcoming post halfway between the police display and the eldest of Dianne's younger sisters, Lourdes, sitting at the front desk with the guest book. She was also in charge of the party helpers, and I asked her to assign guardians to the gingerbread displays.

By my standards, this year's open house was a great party: no one brought us cats, and no one got murdered. None of my exes attended either, unless you count Dianne. Not that she doesn't count, but she's now my business partner in Black Orchid Enterprises and permanent friend. She swished down the gallery hall faster and more graceful than I, even as she carried cups of party punch for us.

As people trundled by and lobbed holiday greetings, I savored my punch and listened to the snips and snatches of conversations. I like to hear what people say when they're not talking to me, mostly complimentary today, as expected from people being fed and receiving presents. I was hoping to hear about the issue that called Officer Al away, but I didn't. I decided I could wait. It's not like it would be good news.

Between new guests, I stole glances at Dianne, now blooming even more gorgeous than the day I met her at the University of Texas freshman mixer. She not only wore the following decade well, she completely rocked it. I knew her heart was a bag of shattered glass, but wasn't everybody's, life being life?

She came to Beauchamp renouncing everything— smoking, bars (except to dance or sing), gaming, social media, dieting, dating, and all but one sugar-free Pepsi per day. That made it hard to buy her Christmas presents. I used to hand her a gift card to her latest online game. Girl was unhappy, my keen intuition told me.

For the past year, she'd thrown herself into making Black Orchid Enterprises a going concern. Somebody had to. Johnny didn't expect or want his cat hospital to be more than part time, and there were not enough ambulances for me to chase, even if I wanted to. So she wrote grants to fund all the service projects we'd rather be doing, and now Johnny is paid to spay, neuter, vaccinate, and shelter local animals, I'm paid to defend immigrants and the indigent in court, and she's paid to do taxes and give financial advice to people who can't afford either.

She and I helped the credit union set up their pay-day loan service that charged only 10% interest as opposed to the typical Texas APR of 640%, like Zippy Bucks out on the highway charges. Rumor has it that Zippy Bucks won't be renewing their lease next year. Dianne and I both considered that more of an achievement than the awards and scholarships moldering in our résumés.

Even this close to the party's end, a steady stream of people poured in, many in groups, the occasion being an occasion for reunions of families and friends, like the sedate group of fifties-plus girlfriends just now tramping through the front door. They exclaimed over the hanging flower baskets on the porch as they signed the guest book.

A soft, happy smile danced over Dianne's features. One of the year's surprise discoveries was her latent love of gardening. Having accepted that kittens and plants mix like oil and water, she embraced gardening on the walls and ceilings with gusto. The porches that ringed the 1897 house on all sides and two stories now sported at least five hanging baskets each. Dianne coaxed the hanging gardens into blazing blooms of pansies, cyclamen, and hellebores in shades from bright red to maroon. Lush, drooping ferns and twining ivy provided the Christmas green. Of course, traditional greenery and lights decked the porch rails, but the flowers made it special.

I told her so.

Her smile flashed just for me. "Everything's better this year, don't you think?"

I agreed. "No one's brought us stray cats, for one."

"No murder for another," said Dianne. She cupped her hands around her punch cup and breathed in the spices.

"It's not over."

"Almost."

An ear-splitting crash—part shatter, part thud—resounded on the far end of the porch.

CHAPTER 2

Dianne and I locked dismayed gazes. In my long-time role of Investigator of Things That Go Bump (yeah, sexist), I headed for the front door in my manliest stride. Because Dianne doesn't put up with that garbage, she was right behind me. So were the guests, now numbering only a quarter of the town's population.

The formerly hanging basket on the far end lay on the porch in pieces. A scarlet pansy raised its drooping head from rubble; the rest lay face down in the dirt. A small cry rose from Dianne's throat.

The only other sound was the steady creak as the second basket from the end swung in a long, slow arc. As it turned, it revealed a creature riding it, with claws clasping the macrame plant hanger—not one Dianne's tías made for her, I hoped. The creature reminded me of a cat, but it had no fur, just pink, wrinkly skin, huge eyes, and ears over a skinny body and legs. While it chomped the ferns, the intruder trained jewel-blue eyes on us and hissed, showing vampire teeth.

Now everybody crowded into the doorway, shoving Dianne and me into the yard. I shivered; the temperature had dropped since the morning. My grandmother at the piano swung into a martial rendition of "Joy to the World," appropriate for this Slayer of Ferns. Grandmother would have remained on the sinking Titanic, but playing "Be My Little Baby Bumble

Bee" instead of "Nearer My God to Thee," because she wouldn't have noticed the ship sinking until her knees got wet.

When she got to "Let Heaven and Nature sing," the cat-like substitute identified with either or both and burst into a primal yowl like I've never heard, even from Dianne's flame point Siamese cat.

"Johnny!" I called as forcefully as I could without raising my voice. I didn't want to frighten the visitor. The situation called for ghostbusters or a vampire hunter—definitely not a lawyer or accountant—but the closest we had was a vet who was also the animal control officer.

The crowd rippled behind me as Johnny pushed to the fore.

"Clear the doorway," he commanded in his vet's soothing voice. "I'd rather guide him into the house."

Not sure we wanted a cross between a vampire and a cat in our home, Dianne and I exchanged alarmed glances. But this was Johnny's gig, and we stepped aside to let everyone through, including our siblings and cousins we'd hired as party helpers. Everyone poured into the front yard with Johnny's glares moving them further away from the house. Dianne and I walked in front of them to enforce the ruling. The party helpers joined in, pretending they'd come outside to help and not gawk, not at all.

The guests shuffled back a few steps while maintaining a running commentary.

"Looks like a plucked chicken."

"In a skin suit that's too big. Look at them wrinkles."

"You sure it's not a bat, with those ears? A great big bat."

"More like that li'l Yoda dude, but pink, not green. Are girl Yodas pink?"

"Can he fly with those ears? They look like wings."

"Biggest swamp rat I ever saw."

"I'll get my gun. That'll take care of him all right."

In a flash, Johnny transformed from Cat(?) Whisperer to black-belt martial artist who's decided it's a good day for you to die. People stepped away from Gun Dude as Johnny turned his head in slow motion. He stared in a way that should have fried the guy where he stood.

"There will be no guns brandished on this property to harm any living creature." Each word burned.

Gun Dude remembered an important appointment and took off in his pickup.

"This is a rare Sphynx cat," Johnny intoned in his softest accents, returning his attention to the rare Sphynx. "Someone paid a lot of money for him and now grieves his loss.

Suddenly interested, Dianne studied the yowling, spitting cat. I figured she was calculating the possibility of a reward. Patrolling the edge of the crowd to force them back further, she murmured, "I didn't know cats came in Pure Ugly."

"Eye of the beholder, sweetie," I whispered as I passed.

Johnny continued his cat whispering murmur as our intern appeared in the doorway. In case Johnny's Zen approach didn't work, Darryl held the animal control officer's chief tool, a five-foot catch pole with a net on the end. His leather gloves came up to his elbows, in case five feet wasn't enough distance. I've seen his expression in photos of young men his age on their way to the war du jour, whether Vietnam for my grandfather's generation, or Afghanistan and Iraq for mine.

The cat growled a low ostinato. We got the crowd quiet enough and far enough away that we could hear Johnny's murmuring, the hanging plant's creaking as it rock-a-byed its shivering burden, and in the distance, Grandmother caressing the piano keys to bring forth "Silent Night." Finding the show dull, some guests drifted off to their cars rather than stand outside in the cold. They had a point.

Dianne moved around the far end of the porch, in case the cat decided to leave that way. I covered the center, in front of our patrolling party elves, in case he came into the front yard. My one hope was that he wouldn't dash into a group of people. His claws were as long as fish hooks, his teeth worthy of his wildcat ancestors.

Some people might have gone inside for cocoa and marshmallows, but they don't live with Dr. John Ky Ly, whose personal goal is to save all the cats in the world. So we hung around.

I'd decided that Johnny was waiting for all the guests to leave, but after losing only another third of our audience, Johnny took one step closer to the Sphynx: the moment of ultimate trust.

That was too much.

With a howl of betrayal or battle cry, the (alleged) cat sprang from his basket and landed on the next one. Dianne shrieked, a mother's cry for her endangered child.

Now at eye level with Johnny, the beast leapt again, this time landing on the floor. His claws scrabbled on the wood as he struggled to gain purchase while making a beeline for the door.

Darryl tensed as his moment arrived. He held the net like he was going to scoop tadpoles in the bayou. The Sphynx didn't slow down, just sailed right over the net and into the house. Alarmed, Darryl stumbled sideways, crashing into decorations before landing on the Pittman & Davis fruit boxes.

I took the porch steps in one leap and burst into the house, with Dianne and the Christmas elves right behind me. She slammed the door and locked it. We blinked and snuffled the grapefruit miasma out of our eyes and noses.

"Go change clothes, Darryl," commanded Johnny. "Citrus upsets the cats."

Dripping grapefruit and orange juice, Darryl staggered to the adjoining cat clinic. I couldn't see the invader, but I saw where he'd been. The gingerbread houses on the gallery-hall's right side looked like Tornado Alley. The piano crooned "O Little Town of Bethlehem." The ginger-bread pieces did indeed lie still.

Johnny folded his arms across his chest. "I'm letting him settle down. He's frightened."

"Do we have enough insurance for that?" I asked Dianne.

"Cookies aren't insurable," she replied, wincing as the turrets on an artful castle went flying.

I surveyed the long gallery, full of more treasures than cookies. I sidled to my office door and shut it. "Normally I'd say we lock the doors, go to a hotel, and call in the crime scene cleaners. But we're hosting a concert here Monday night, and we've promised to return all the gingerbread displays that people have worked on for weeks—Sunday for the churches, Monday for the businesses—and we don't want to hand them a bag of crumbs. And there's more in this house for a rampaging cat to destroy. But it's your house, Johnny. Or rather, your grandmother's."

We all turned to look at Mrs. Ly ensconced in her red velvet throne near the fireplace. Her long-time friend, Leigh Brandon, sat next to her in a similar chair, but smaller and gold. The gallery furniture, now on the verge of antique, came from Mrs. Ly's grandparents. Miss Leigh's daughters Claire and Melanie and their children huddled close, staring in horror at the galloping cat-monster.

A sprinkling of guests remained, those who hadn't rushed outside to see the invasion. I recognized some as people who wanted to take their gingerbread creation with them at day's end. I winced. I hadn't counted on handing out the bags of crumbs so soon.

Resigned as only a mother, grandmother, and school nurse could be, Mrs. Ly waved a hand. "Like I told you when you got your chemistry set for your tenth birthday, John Ky, you clean up whatever mess you make."

To prove my point, the cat plowed through the floor-to-cathedral-ceiling Christmas tree, which shivered, but stayed upright. Ornaments on the lower branches fell off, but they hit the tree skirt and presents.

Emerging on the opposite side of the tree, he headed for the food tables in front of the back windows. Our party helpers screeched and spread themselves in front of and across the food in dramatic gestures worthy of a battle movie. They would have looked more heroic without the Santa hats.

"I hope that cat doesn't go upstairs." Dianne moved in that direction. "Think what he could do to our bedrooms."

She stopped when the last house tour thundered down the stairs.

"The cats got out!" shouted the tour guide, Dianne's brother Zap.

Sure enough, ahead of the herd scampered our four house kittens, the ones we received as babies during last year's party. Now they were rangy teenagers, the three tabbies always ready for chaos, and the dainty flame point Siamese looking adorably confused, as though searching for her one brain cell.

Dianne named the white kitten Nevada, Spanish for snowy, but she doesn't explain that anymore, now that Nevada has turned toasty gold. Though not an honors student at Feline U, Nevada had mastered one concept at least: mine. She streaked across the room but pulled up short, out of the new cat's reach, where she screamed to the heavens that this house was her house, only hers. Her golden fur fluffed out like a scrub brush. The tabbies seemed mildly interested, being used to the procession of cats through the shelter and clinic, where they had free run. But they played along with Nevada's threats, gradually ringing the Sphynx and declaiming threats. The newcomer spun in the center and hissed at each in turn.

"These are our cats," said Johnny. "They should respond to us."

What a weird thing for a vet to say. No cat ever respected should, certainly not ours. The tabbies raised the threat level to growl. Nevada screamed louder and longer, stalking the interloper, who backed towards the tables holding the gingerbread village. She pounced, and the Sphynx jumped straight up on the table.

Grandmother's carols still twinkled from the piano. My grandfather stepped in front of it, his jaw set. He earned medals for his bravery in Vietnam, but he looked baffled in the face of a house pet invasion.

The back door flew open to admit Officer Alejandro Quintanilla-Villanueva. The reaction from my sheltered childhood was, "Good! The police are here!" As an adult, I just about trusted our friend Officer Al not to pull out his gun and start shooting, but no part of my mother's teaching included Cupcake the Wonder Dog, Officer Al's demented-looking husky.

Cupcake is a highly trained dog. She ignores that training when she feels like it, which is why she's Officer Al's personal pet instead of an employed police dog. She seized the opportunity she's never allowed when she comes to Johnny's Friday night community dinners—to play with the cats.

We're almost sure she wouldn't hurt them, but that uncertainty is why she's never allowed up close and personal. She bounded after Ginger Tom, the tabby nearest the back door. Ginger squalled and leapt on the piano.

He flattened himself enough to squeeze under the lid, propped open at the lowest level. Looking triumphant, Grandfather shut the lid, trapping the cat, who ended Grandmother's phrase with "How still we see thee Miaou!"

"Cupcake!" shouted the officer.

He was ignored.

"Jay!" Grandmother shouted, louder than I'd ever heard her sweet Southern voice.

She was ignored.

"I didn't hurt him," Grandfather protested, gesturing to the yowls coming from inside the piano.

"The piano has just been tuned! We have a concert on Monday!"

Intern Darryl returned from the clinic with his arms full of cat carriers and a water spray bottle. He grabbed Ginger Tom from the guts of the piano and stuffed him in a carrier. He squirted water on the tabby nearest his feet, who darted across the room to join her brother. Dianne's youngest sisters jumped into a zone defense to herd them into the nearest bedroom. Tima and Juke had been starters for the Santa María Guadalupe College Prep basketball team, and it showed.

They crouched lower than they ever had on the court as they swiped wide at the two cats, quite a feat in dress shoes, especially Tima's four-inch spikes. Juke was handicapped by her embroidered circle skirt dragging the floor. Tima's red bandage dress offered a different challenge. I admired her form, thighs almost vertical, knees skimming the floor. Her playing form, I meant.

Every lunge forced the cats closer to the bedroom but made them madder. Finally, Juke drove down the middle, this time catching her heel in her skirt as she scooped the tabbies into the room. Tima slammed the door shut. Juke crashed into it. The crowd went wild; the cats on the other side of the door also.

"Touchdown!" I shouted. Oops, wrong sportsball.

The Sphynx ran to the back and scrambled across the backdoor welcome desk—and my sister Merry—before throwing himself at the plate glass window next to the back door. He hit it with a thunk and a howl. To save him from falling, Merry grabbed him, but he spun like a barrel and launched himself out of her arms.

Darryl chuckled as his phone captured the event. "This is going on social media for sure."

The Sphynx dashed back up the gallery through the confections with Nevada in hot pursuit. Leaving crumbs in their wake, they clashed over the gingerbread cathedral. It soared, if not to the heavens, at least high above the rest of the village, though it was getting shorter by the second as the two cats tumbled. Their tails lashed, one a thin whip, the other a golden plume. Fur literally flew in puffs, all of it from Nevada, because the Sphynx had none. They looked like angel and demon, battling for the soul of the church. The Sphynx howled as Nevada sunk her teeth into his bare shoulder. Flying buttresses, steeple, and rose window crashed in shards on the floor.

Johnny emerged from another bedroom with two afghans knitted by his Aunt Chana. Dianne and I took one; Darryl put his phone away and took the other end of Johnny's. We crept toward the combatants and waited for an opening. They'd have to separate before we could contain them. When the Sphynx flipped over backwards—I hoped somebody filmed that—and took a second to spit out another mouthful of fur, we dived in, wrapping each target in an Afghan. Nevada and Dianne screeched as she ran for her office. Nevada's claws went right through the fabric.

Johnny ran for the clinic with his lurching bundle. It keened a cry of the damned so loud and low that the floor vibrated. The piano strings hummed, and half the Cortez family made the sign of the cross.

As Darryl raised his phone to record the gingerbread destruction, he declared, "Only one name for him. Godzilla."

I held my hand out for his phone after he finished recording his panorama.

Officer Al held tight to Cupcake, lunging in the belief that everyone was having a good time. "Johnny, I need you in the back lot. And I want to talk to anyone who met with Guy Randall."

Johnny froze. There was only one reason Officer Al would need the Assistant Justice of the Peace, and it wasn't for Cupcake's shots.

Mutterings about Guy Randall drifted across the room. He was part of the group I'd seen paying tribute to Mrs. Ly. They were old friends from high school. One was now Miss Leigh's son-in-law. One was a Beauchamp wheeler and dealer who claimed to be a real estate magnate. No one knew what Guy claimed to be; he left Beauchamp shortly after high school.

Dianne and I were both wrong. This party brought us both a new cat and a murder.

Everyone looked at everyone until Miss Leigh's daughter Melanie offered, "I think he came alone. He said he didn't have family. He laughed about that."

Johnny resumed his progress to the clinic and put his foot in a metaphorical social bucket. "So he's dead. Do I need my special equipment?"

Officer Al probably answered Johnny, but I couldn't hear it over the explosion of reactions, some words, some just sounds. I could distinguish only what Johnny's little sister, standing next to me, said.

"So there is a God," muttered Sophie Thi.

CHAPTER 3

With a resigned glare at Johnny, Al raised his voice, his official one. "I need everyone to stay until I talk to you."

"We've got ballet tickets in Austin," moaned one of the better dressed guests.

"A man is dead," stated Officer Al, who hadn't intended to break it to us in that way. "We need to find out why."

He is always sure that everyone has the same community spirit that he does. Or else he learned in police school to proclaim it.

Chantal, ever the Brave Little Toaster, reassured the remaining guests, their faces now Christmas green at the damage to their creations and the possibility of being part of a murder investigation.

"We'll spend tomorrow repairing them so they'll be ready to display on Monday. We have lots of photos. We'll have a big workshop of elves to help because our families are staying the night. Johnny, I'll help you start the gingerbread in a few minutes. That way it'll be cool in the morning." If Chantal had been on the Titanic, everyone would have made their own little lifeboats and sailed to safety.

She makes everyone something for Christmas, like the diagonally striped red tie I was wearing with my pale green dress shirt, the horizontally striped forest green tie that Johnny wore with his green lab coat, and the red and green vertically striped tie around Darryl's neck.

"What is this morning of which you speak?" demanded Dianne, in a firm but soft voice as she eyed Godzilla's lashing tail. "I've promised to go to eleven o'clock Mass with my mother."

Soothing the furious cat, Johnny backed toward the clinic door. "I'll start the gingerbread as soon as I get him settled."

Miss Leigh touched my arm and murmured, "May I talk to you, JD?"

We edged into my office. I threw a backward glance at Sophie Thi, scowling with her arms crossed over her chest like an Asian Texas Lisbet Salander.

"JD, do I need to pay you any more to act as Melanie's attorney—Lem's too, of course—during questioning?" She wrinkled her nose, like she'd stepped on something soft in the pasture. When I didn't answer, she continued, "We already have a contract with you for my business. Is that sufficient to cover this matter?"

"It's not a good idea to represent multiple people at once," I hedged.

"I'm sure it would be fine for the initial questioning," she persisted in her Southern honeyed voice. "We could make other arrangements later, if necessary. I'd want you to stay with Melanie, of course."

It struck me how much of Southern society runs on the assumed agreement "of course." I glanced over her head at Sophie Thi, who now stubbed her boot toe into the carpet.

"It's not a good idea. Also, I need to check whether I have a previous commitment. I'll get back to you as soon as I can."

Thunder in her face told me that time better be measured in seconds. I excused myself and made a beeline for the back door, now opening to readmit Officer Al and Johnny. As I detoured around Sophie Thi, Chantal and Darryl blocked my path.

"You're going to be our attorney?" demanded Chantal, fingernails digging into my arm.

"It's an employment benefit, right?" asked Darryl as he squeezed my opposite elbow.

"What do you need an attorney for?" I countered.

"The police are going to question us. We're the only Black people in the room. You know they're going to figure we did it," Chantal whispered.

"Even though you never met the guy before today?" I asked, not wanting to point out that Al was Latino, like at least half of our guests.

Darryl shook his head. "Don't matter. That's how it works. Ask my cousin. He's serving time for burglary on a house he never saw before in his life. Also, can I have my phone back?"

"Don't worry. I'll take care of you," I promised, running through my mental contact list as I handed him his phone and disentangled myself from the conversation. "Can you send me and Chantal the reel of Godzilla and Merry?"

Lourdes Cortez, who'd been at the front door welcoming desk, accosted me as I reached the looming Christmas tree. We were glad to have her in our holiday-palooza because she assisted her mother in their event-planning firm. Her brow furrowed in worry, not something I've seen often.

"JD, that man who died, he's the one who kept bothering the elves all day."

I waited. *Bothering* could mean anything from a misogynistic remark to full on criminal assault. This was the first I'd heard of it, and I felt a caveman-type protectiveness, not that I didn't think any of the elves—Cortez sisters, cousins, my sisters, and Johnny's—couldn't handle any situation, but they shouldn't have to.

"They're wondering if they should say anything to the police, now that he's dead. Tima and Juke are particularly upset. He wouldn't leave them alone and got pretty graphic."

Tima and Juke Cortez were one year older and younger than my own sisters. I could see where this was going.

"Cherry whacked his nose with a food tray, claiming it was an accident, you know."

Great. Now one of my sisters was involved, and I was betting that Merry was too.

"Could you tell them what to say? Maybe sit with them when they're questioned?"

"I'll take care of it," I assured Lourdes as I dove across the last stretch to where Johnny and Officer Al argued *sotto voce* by the back door. Johnny's face held no expression as usual, unless "even more blank" is an expression, but Al's brown face was turning red.

I arrived in time to hear Johnny say, "My duty as Assistant Justice of the Peace is to declare death and make recommendations for further investigation, if called for. We agree that the victim is dead, probably from the stab wound, as evidenced by the blood on his shirt. We agree that an autopsy is the best way to make this determination, and I will so order after consultation with the county attorney. I expect the investigation to proceed appropriately, and I have no further duties."

"But you've always helped with investigations! I owe my last promotion to you."

Cupcake added her voice to his and whined in her throat. I hoped it wouldn't turn into a growl. I've seen what she can do to a bad guy. I didn't want Johnny to become the bad guy. That brought a weird picture into my mind—Who would win? Martial artist or attack dog?

Johnny replied in his flat voice, "The sheriff's office frequently tells me I overstep my bounds. I'm trying to do better. I'll share the photos I took like I always do."

Having decided that Cupcake would have the advantage in a fight because Johnny would be trying not to hurt her—his normal attitude in a fight is "It's a good day to die and I'm taking you with me"—I interrupted their standoff. "Johnny, can we talk in your office?"

"Certainly. I'm done with my part of the investigation." He threaded his way through the bystanders to his office, a tiny room with doors to both the clinic and the gallery. He punched in the unlock code—we have limits to this open house concept—and we shut out the party behind us, though not in front of us, because the connecting door to the clinic was open, and Godzilla was in full feline operatic mode, backed up by the chorus of our boarder and foster cats. Johnny went to comfort him but jumped back when the cat hissed and swatted through the cage bars. Johnny moved to the next cage and stroked its calico occupant though the bars.

I followed close behind. I didn't know how much time I had. "Johnny, Miss Leigh wants me to represent her family during police questioning. So do Chantal, Darryl, the Cortez elves, and probably my sister, though she hasn't said, but I've been tap dancing with them all because I thought you might want me to represent your sister." I told him what Sophie Thi said. "The others are just scared, but she might actually have a motive."

He stroked the calico's jaw once more with two fingers before standing straight to look up into my eyes. "No. I don't want you to represent Sophie Thi. I want you to represent me."

CHAPTER 4

I leaned against the cages and shut my eyes. An orange tabby cat poked my shoulder, and a tortie, my pant leg. When she switched to claws, I stood up and backed off.

"You killed him?" I asked.

"No. I would have done a better job. But I see that I have a motive, and I don't know if I can prove an alibi."

"Alibi? You were giving a party. And what—"

"Was I in someone's sight every minute? I gave tours of the clinic and the shelter."

"And chased down a wild cat, though I don't see how you can do all those things and commit murder too. But what—"

"That's why I recused myself from the investigation. Even though I'm not involved with his death, my investigating it would have a bad appearance."

"Yes. But. Why?" I shouted in whispers, mindful of party guests and possible police on the other side of the wall, even though a trio of Siamese kittens was screaming about losing their mittens or something worse. For a second, I felt a kinship with Johnny's middle school classmates who tried to put his head in the toilet after gym class. Once. He was already well on his way to a black belt. He was as proud of his three-day suspension from school (fought and overturned by his parents, but not before three days had passed) as he was any of his truckload of academic honors.

"You know Sophie Thi and I have had a difficult relationship."

I nodded, remembering her storming through last year's open house after the Ly family insisted that she come support her brother's new business.

"This year we met in Austin for coffee every quarter, whether we wanted to or not. That was her rule. She appears to have to force herself to achieve goals. To avoid us glowering across the table while the coffee cooled, she brought an agenda for discussion."

"Sounds like Dianne's Life by Spreadsheet."

"It did seem familiar in that way, but it was useful to get people talking who don't talk. We'd each say something from adulthood that the other didn't know, that being defined as post-college. Then we'd share something from childhood that the other didn't know. Finally, she made a random generator of shared occasions from our childhoods, and for the one selected, we'd each recite our memory of it, which often differed."

Anxious to return to my gallery of clients, I glanced toward the hall as Johnny crossed the room to soothe the kittens.

"Visiting our grandparents in Beauchamp was always a refuge for me, but Sophie Thi seemed to have a love-hate relationship with the place. She didn't want to be left out, but she didn't like going to school with Grandmother or to the restaurant with Grandfather, like I did. When she was very small, Melanie Brandon babysat her a few times, but soon she wouldn't stay with Melanie. Miss Leigh or Grandmother's other friends would look after her, and she didn't mind staying with Claire, when Claire was old enough to babysit. Sophie Thi was always difficult, so no one thought anything of it." He stopped to sigh, while I looked at my watch.

"When Melanie came to Gregg House to babysit, she'd invite her boyfriend Lem—her husband now—and he'd bring his friends. While Melanie and Lem were doing couple things in another room, the friends would..." Vocabulary failed him. "One friend was Guy Randall, the murder victim."

Now I remembered how she'd ducked away from the three bros. "Johnny, she's got just as much motive as you do, so unless the murderer was tall and right-handed and she's left-handed and only five-foot-two, she's a suspect."

Johnny thought about it. "I couldn't see the wound clearly. I can't do a thorough investigation on a body lying on the ground. She's ambidextrous, preferring one hand for some actions, the other for others. I'm not sure which she'd use to stab someone—or how expert she'd be."

"I'm glad it didn't come up in your childhood. She still needs counsel, and I shouldn't represent you both."

"Really? Then go with which one of us is interviewed first." He reached in the cage to pull out all three kittens, who swarmed in his arms and snuggled. "I'll stay with the cats. I can be useful here."

Across the room, the bare-naked cat screamed his audition for Cats Bust Glass or something similar. I shook my head at his bulging eyes, huge ears, and rippling pink skin and turned my gaze back to the darling fluffy kittens. "Johnny, that cat is not only the ugliest cat I've ever seen but is in competition for the ugliest animal."

"That's because you weren't a biology major. Besides, you have to look at his soul."

Godzilla turned around, the better to pee on the floor from his cage. As the stinging stink of cat urine rose in the air, I felt I'd seen and smelled enough of his soul. I returned to the gallery.

Claire Brandon, one hand gripping the piano lid, was talking to Pastor Nathan of Beauchamp First Baptist Church by the piano. She didn't seem to enjoy the discussion, but she, being her mother's daughter, made polite excuses as she gracefully intercepted me.

"JD, could I talk to you a few minutes? Does our contract include your legal services in matters besides my mother's finances?"

After an acknowledging smile, I took a step back and a deep breath. I announced in my courtroom voice, "All of my clients, family, and friends who want me to act for them today, please gather in my office immediately."

I pointed to the round office at the front on my right, but the herd didn't seem to need directions. The gallery cleared in seconds. I hoped I could get inside the office too. My grandfather left my grandmother, noodling Christmas carols at the piano, to join me. "JD, do you need help?"

"Indeed I do. The police will start interviews for their murder investigation any minute, and four groups of people want my advice."

"I didn't think your main focus was criminal defense."

"It's not, though I might be getting a crash apprenticeship. Will you talk to some of these people for me?"

He nodded and began a stately progression to the office. The remaining few guests, those with ballet tickets and other plans, milled about, stress eating and drinking.

"How long do we have to stay here?" demanded the ballet goer. He looked like a "drag-ee," what we called the accompanying partner who'd rather be anywhere but a particular cultural event. But that didn't mean he was going to put up with being late to it.

"I have no idea." I raised my voice again. "Any lawyers onsite?"

Shaking heads told me no, and no one stepped forward. A middle-aged woman in a Christmas-striped pantsuit asked, "What's going to happen? Do we need to find a lawyer? How can we get someone on a Saturday afternoon?"

I tried for a reassuring smile as I moved away. "Technically, no. The police will do their initial interviews, mostly wanting to know if anyone saw anything relevant and if you have some association with the victim. If you'd prefer to wait until you do have an attorney with you, you can tell them that."

"We don't even know who the victim is."

"How do we know what's relevant?"

"We don't know when it happened."

"What *did* happen?"

Their random paths got wider and more focused on the exits. Lourdes moved back to her post near the front door, and I gestured to Dianne's brother Zap, hanging out between the Christmas tree and the back door reception desk, where my sister Merry sat, anxious. She was the worrying twin.

"Zap, would you keep the populace from leaving?" I asked.

He looked thoughtful.

"Don't get physical. If they insist on going, get their names and contact info, a photo if possible. We'll turn it over to the police. I don't mind if they know that. Text Johnny and tell him to guard the front door."

Merry sniffed. "You don't think I can handle that?"

"I do. But Zap looks more threatening than you do, particularly when he glowers."

"I can glower," agreed Zap, pulling himself up to his full height and folding his arms over his chest. He has some kind of parks management degree and works for the City of Dallas parks system, with enough outdoor work to make him buff and red-gold bronze.

"I'm taller than Johnny," huffed Merry. "I could sit at the front."

"Most people know about his black belt, though. Any elf not in my office can join Johnny."

"No one will get by us," Zap proclaimed with exquisite tact. He did not pat her hand.

With five guests stalking me, I made a last lunge for my office as Grandmother twinkled her way through "I Wonder as I Wander." Normally my office felt large and luxurious, but Dianne and Chantal had to pull me far enough into the room for Darryl to shut the door behind me.

Getting to my desk was hopeless, even if three elves—Cherry, Tima, and Juke—weren't sitting on it. So I just drew a deep breath, which brought me even more uncomfortably close to Dianne, and declared, "So everybody I've ever spoken to wants me as their attorney. That can't be done, but my grandfather, former U.S. Attorney Jay Thompson, and I will sit in on as many police interviews as we can today. We'll then advise you what kind of future representation you need. We'll try to conduct a private interview with each of you before the police start theirs."

My grandfather, elegant in the antique red velvet client chair halfway across the room, nodded his white mane in a masterful way that I really should practice. I've no idea how he got to that chair. I could barely squeeze in the door.

Sophie Thi shifted in her perch on the windowsill behind my desk. The afternoon sun behind her created an ominous aura as she drawled in a carrying voice, "I guess you want us to confess to the murder?"

CHAPTER 5

The room fell silent when Sophie Thi raised her voice. I was discovering that response was typical. On her right, Melanie stepped away while dragging her two youngest children with her. The move brought her closer to her husband Lem. He took another three steps away for good measure, followed by his two older sons.

Why did people bring their children to a legal conference? Melanie had all four of hers. In the opposite corner by the bookcases, behind the antique globe that hid a drinks cabinet, Claire Brandon stood with her arm around her daughter Harmony. Pastor Nathan stood an ambiguous distance away, not belonging anywhere. He scowled at Claire when he thought she wasn't looking. She wrinkled her nose at him when his gaze was elsewhere.

In front of Sophie in another red velvet client chair, Lourdes Cortez widened her eyes and looked down. The three elves on my desk turned their heads in slow motion to gawk and then snapped back to the front, their expressions trying to hide their jealousy over what Sophie Thi could get away with and they couldn't.

At least it gave me dead time to respond. "Not unless you actually did so. Even if you did, what I want you to do is to say you can't answer questions on advice of counsel. Yes, I'm counsel and I'm sitting right there, but you can answer questions if and when your official attorney thinks it's a good idea. The part about 'can be used against you in a court of law' is a promise—whatever you say will be used against you, so it's best to say nothing. However, you need to tell me or my grandfather exactly what your involvement is with the victim and your movements today."

Dianne offered her office to my grandfather and wiggled out of the room to set it up. Since most of her wiggling was against me, my voice rose a few steps as I barked out names of the first interviewees. I had to clear a path for them and those on the B list to leave, leaning over the drinks globe as I did so. I snagged Lourdes before she got out the door and asked her to help Johnny staff the front desk, like Merry and Zap were doing at the back. Since she was reporting second-hand events and didn't know the victim, I didn't think she'd be long with Grandfather, and I trusted her more than I trusted Johnny, at least in the tact department.

Dianne trying to re-enter the room clogged the exodus briefly—What if Moses and the Israelites had met commuters returning to Egypt in the Red Sea?—but eventually I was behind my desk with Dianne, Chantal, and Darryl in the client chairs in front of me. As I wiped off the desk and returned my tchotchkes to their proper places, if you define legal paraphernalia as "cheap stuff more decorative than functional," which I do—except for my great-grandfather's nameplate, a gift from my grandfather. I was glad he got to sit in front of it and see its place in my life.

Dianne flipped open her laptop and fluttered her fingers over the keys. "I'll take notes."

"Thanks." Maybe I should have wondered what she was up to, but there was just as much of a chance that she wanted to be helpful as any nefarious reason. For sure, I knew she wouldn't want to be left out of anything, except viewing the body. I did wonder if I should have seen Chantal and Darryl separately, like I planned to do with everyone else. "If you two would rather talk to me separately, that's fine. I don't think you have any relevant evidence, but if so . . ."

"JD, being Black is relevant enough," snapped Chantal.

"I know," I agreed, jumping in fast before she could prove it to me again. "So we're going to do our best to provide real evidence. We're dealing with Officer Al here, and he's been fair to us before."

"Yeah, but—" Darryl objected.

I kept talking. "I'm making an assumption neither of you ever saw the victim before today and didn't interact with him much during the party."

Darryl threw up his hands. "I probably took his picture. I took everybody's picture, especially if they got near the gingerbread houses. Is that interaction? What are we going to do about those broken ones? How are we ever going to get them repaired in time? Besides, I don't even know who you're talking about."

"I don't either," grumped Chantal. "But my only interactions were with trays of food and the girls who should have been putting them out instead of chatting up the guests, so I'm saying No."

"Guy Randall," I said. "I never saw him before today. He came late, or I didn't see him until late, and he hung out with the Quistons, Miss Leigh's daughter and her husband, you know."

"The husband mostly, I think, if that's the guy I think he is," said Darryl. "Melanie kept giving them this sour look and moving off. I didn't think anything of it. She does that to her mother and sister too, not to mention everybody else. Besides, her sourpuss face would spoil the photos."

Dianne had pulled up a photo by then and turned her computer so Chantal and Darryl could see. The door dragons hadn't finished the task yet, but they were digitizing the guest book and including photos. Darryl nodded in confirmation of his story, and Chantal shook her head. "He never came into the kitchen, and that's where I was, except when I was singing."

"Lourdes tells me he was hitting on the elves," I offered.

Chantal's eyes blazed. "Oh he was, was he? He better be glad he's dead then, cuz I would string him up so he'd sing countertenor the rest of his miserable celibate existence. Why didn't they tell me?"

"They're capable young women who can take care of themselves. Tima and Juke did tell Lourdes, and Cherry hit him with a tray."

"Hope it was hot food full of spices that won't wash out," grumbled Chantal. "Still wish I'd got to talk to him."

"Me too," Dianne's voice was gritty and grim at the thought of her sisters in peril. "Darryl, I'm sending you a template of my spreadsheet so you can take notes for Mr. Thompson."

"And when you get a minute, could you tag Randall in any photos you took?" I asked.

"You folks ever heard of the Thirteenth Amendment? Slavery and all that? We studied it this semester. I took a couple quintillion photos for this gig," Darryl complained.

"Slavery doesn't apply when you're on overtime," said Dianne. "I'm sure other elves can do it if you don't want to. My cousin Pilar is majoring in graphic design."

"No, overtime's cool. Think I might be close to double time for this week." He slouched out the door like he didn't care.

Dianne and I barely had time to exchange a speaking look before Sophie Thi barreled in and plopped herself in a client chair. Her feet didn't touch the floor. The massive 1940s chair made her look even more like a little girl—Manic Pixie Dreamgirl crossed with Alice in Nightmareland, but still a girl.

I tried to be smooth. "Sophie Thi, how can I help you?"

"Duh, isn't it part of my elvish duty to get accused of murder? My brother texted me and told me to get over here." She swung her legs back and forth, one at a time. Red stripes. Green stripes.

"I—or my grandfather—will come to the police interview with you, if you like. Consider it a benefit of working for the firm, if only for a day."

She shrugged and nodded at the same time. Our Marvelous Dianne slapped a basic contract on the desk in front of her, and Sophie Thi scooted forward and flicked a pen across the bottom of it. If Chantal would have us all making our own lifeboats on the *Titanic*, Dianne would have the supplies gathered and distributed and work sessions scheduled.

As much as we bicker over spontaneity versus organization, Dianne's organization gives my life room for spontaneity. Spontaneous cooking and housecleaning mean you do little of either. I must remember to express my appreciation; I'll put that on the calendar she says I should keep better.

Meanwhile, Johnny's sister sat before me, still swinging a red-striped leg, then a green-striped leg.

"Let's see: you are Sophie Thi Ly, sister of Johnny, daughter of Mark Loc Ly and Solange Vercher, granddaughter of Debbie and Ky Ly. Your profession is?"

"I'm an influencer. You can find me as @SophieT. I use just the initial because I get tired of pronouncing my name for people."

"Ah. Your marketing degree from Princeton must be useful in that line of work."

She wiggled forward and planted her feet on the floor. "Just to be clear, I could sell enough steaming hot cow-patty coffee at the Beauchamp July 4 picnic to cover my expenses for the next year."

"I haven't any doubt of it." I wanted to see what she'd offer me before I told her what I'd heard. Over the backdrop of Dianne's clicking keys, I asked, "What was your relationship with the victim, Guy Randall?"

She scooted back and rolled her eyes back to gaze at the ceiling, full of curlicues and other decor. "I hit him in the nuts when I was five. Does that count?"

Dianne stopped typing. Johnny having prepared me, I kept a neutral tone. "I wouldn't call that a relationship, and I'm sorry that happened to you. I'm assuming he deserved that blow."

"I thought so. Melanie was supposed to be babysitting me, but she invited her boyfriend Lem over, and of course his buddies came too. You always saw them together. While Melanie and Lem got on with ruining their lives, Guy and Doug were supposed to be looking after me. At first they just tickled me until I screamed. Then Guy did things that didn't make me scream, but I didn't like it. So I grabbed Grandaddy's bronze statue of Phat Ba Quan Am—that's the Vietnamese Kwan Yin—and whacked him as hard and as high as I could. He screeched louder than me, which is saying something, and

Melanie and Lem came out of their love nest. Lem laughed. That sound is burned indelibly in my hippocampus. Isn't that a great phrase?"

"It is. Did you tell anyone?"

"I sure didn't tell Grandaddy about using his Goddess of Compassion as a weapon of war."

"I don't know how your grandfather would have felt, but I'm sure the goddess approved of defending a child."

"I told Granny Deb I hated Melanie and was never staying with her again. Granny Deb could always read between the lines. After that, I didn't stay with a babysitter much, or I stayed with an adult friend of Granny Deb. Later I figured out one of those friends was a therapist. I thought we were just playing dollies. I hate dollies, but I tried to be polite. Do I tell the police all this?"

"I wouldn't lead with it, if we were saying anything. The short version might be that you met him as a child but haven't seen him since until today."

She nodded.

"But you didn't speak with him?"

She nodded again.

"Because you were busy with your duties, which claimed all your attention."

"That's not laying it on too thick?"

"You looked busy to me. Did you see him interacting with other guests?"

"Being too busy with my duties, I saw only his dude bros from high school, Lem and then later Dopey Doug. I made sure my duties didn't cross their path. Sourpuss Melanie flounced off after barely a word with him when he arrived. Her face could curdle beer."

I didn't bother with scientific accuracy. Besides, I agreed with her. "About what time did you first notice them?"

"About halfway through this geologic age of an afternoon, because your sister said something about being halfway done, and I thought, only a million years to go, but then I saw Guy and gagged. Then worse, Dopey

Doug showed up, and I don't know when anybody left, if they did. I guess Guy did, though."

Dianne turned her laptop around to show Sophie Thi a photo of the three bros, fortunately not laughing, instead with expressions like they got the candy with the Jordan almond (never my fave). Guy was an unremarkable beer-gutted middle-class white guy, like Lem; Dopey Doug was one of the suits I'd noticed earlier. I wondered what lifted Doug to a better destiny than the others found. I wondered too what Doug's full name was, but Sophie Thi hadn't been formally introduced.

To wrap up a harrowing interview, I asked, "Pretend you're the police, and tell me if there's any reason they would think you committed this murder, other than this history, which I view as something for your defense attorney to manage. Our attitude is going to be that you met him once twenty years ago and not since, not that he inflicted a lasting psychological wound on you."

She lifted both legs and cocked her toes back, the better to study her short boots. "Well, I've had lots of therapy. I'm a therapy kind of girl. Mostly I can meet my abusers without killing them. As my therapist—I forget which one—says, make sure you're responding to the now, not the then. But why the police might think I killed this guy—" From the side of her left boot, she pulled out a short, skinny knife from its hidden sheath. "I'm ready to."

I tried to hide my shock. "I did hear you say 'So there is a God,' after his death was announced. But as your attorney, I won't say that to anyone else."

"Thanks. I carry a weapon, but I use it for defense, not offense. And I stopped praying for his death by torture a long time ago. Therapy, remember? Also I quit praying."

I focused my phone on the knife and asked, "Mind?" She gave the same shrug-nod, and I tapped a shot and sent it to Johnny. "And would you mind if I kept it?"

"Yeah, I would. Why?" All traces of young innocence vanished from her twisted features.

"So we look like we're cooperating with the investigation, putting away a possible murder weapon in as pristine a condition as possible. Could you put it in this bag?" I held out one of Johnny's evidence bags.

Her hand (left) clutched the knife, and I thought she was going to throw it at my throat. Instead she took the bag and inserted the knife with exaggerated care. She held the bag between thumb and middle finger (on her right hand) to give it back.

"I'm not going to offer it to them," I promised.

"And you'll defend me to the death, since you took my weapon, right?"

"Right."

"Just one more thing."

We both twitched at Dianne's Columbo-like interjection. I looked away from Johnny's response on my screen: a shrug emoji.

Dianne asked, "Did you let the other elves know?"

"No. I didn't care if anyone waited on those jerks. They look like they can find their own food and drink, no prob."

"But the elves could have helped screen you from the men that made you uncomfortable."

Sophie Thi looked blank. "They'd do that? They don't even know me."

Dianne said, "At least for today, you're one of my sisters and cousins, hermanas y primas, and an employee of Black Orchid Enterprises. I assure you they would."

"They adopted my sisters into that tribe ten years ago," I added. "It's not just the Cortez family."

"If you'd said something, they could have protected you, and they could have been prepared for him. Instead he hit on my sisters, and JD's sister dumped a tray of food on him."

Sophie Thi looked ashamed. "Literally, really, I never thought of that. I'm not good with the family-friend thing."

I stood up to end the interview. "You're good enough to have coffee with Johnny to mend your relationship. You came up with good questions."

"I'd call it creating, since we didn't have much of a relationship to begin with. My therapist—you seeing a pattern here?—thought it would be good for me and helped me come up with the questions." Sophie Thi stood also and adjusted the position of her cross-body envelope purse. She took a step towards the door but turned back to say, "I couldn't wait to get away from all of Johnny's animals, but in college I missed having pets. So I got this betta fish, little blue thing with wavy fins. I should only have such good hair. It just sat in a transparent bowl the size of a big coffee cup. Maybe turned around sometimes. Just stared. Or contemplated. I couldn't tell. I named it Johnny."

CHAPTER 6

It took a few minutes to round up the Brandon clan and separate the mothers from young children. With a murderer on the loose, they didn't feel safe with their kids out of their sight, but I didn't think the kids needed to hear details that might upset them. Or not. You never know with some kids. So we settled Matthew, Mark, and Luke Quiston with Zap and Merry by the backdoor and Mary Quiston and her older cousin Harmony Brandon, whom she adored, by the front door with Lourdes and Johnny.

With Miss Leigh and her daughters in the client chairs and Lem Quiston eyeing the folding chair brought in for him, I started into my speech about not being able to represent them all but would accompany them to their police interviews today.

Lem interrupted after the first sentence. "I don't need representation. That's for guilty people. I'm going back to Miss Leigh's house. My best friend from high school was murdered, and I don't need all this crap."

"Lem, the police will want to talk to you," objected Melanie.

"They know where to find me." He headed for the door.

"We're putting together a timeline to help with the investigation," I called after him.

Dianne added, "We know from the guest book when you arrived, one of the first arrivals. When did you first see Mr. Randall?"

He leaned hard against the doorjamb. "Before I had time to die of boredom, so not long after that."

She persisted, "And then Mr. Severn joined you. Do you know what time? Or what time they left?"

"No, I don't," he shouted. "We were going to do something together tonight or tomorrow, but now we won't ever."

His wife flinched. Her mother sat up even straighter and turned a steely gaze on him.

"Lem!" cried Melanie as he opened the door. More determined than fast, she pursued him.

I tried to soothe the remaining angry women. "As he said, the police can find him if he just goes across the street. Miss Leigh, why don't I talk to you first and then Claire? By then Melanie should be back."

Claire struggled to flash us all a smile as she departed to join her daughter and niece. I wondered again, as I did every time I saw the whole family together, how Southern-sweet Miss Leigh bore and bred the cheery bohemian Claire and the rigid, miserable Melanie.

"I still don't see why you can't represent the whole family," complained Miss Leigh, though in sugary tones.

"Because it might not be in everyone's best interests," I replied, done with tiptoeing. "A lawyer needs to put the interests of his client above all else—and if one of you killed him, another drove the getaway car, and the third watched the whole thing, each of you need a different defense."

"That's a terrible thing to say! Of course my family had nothing to do with murder," she exclaimed, dropping the sugar.

"I hope not, but neither the police nor I have eliminated anyone yet. Let's see if we can. You and your family arrived first, as usual, but last year Melanie's husband wasn't with her, so his presence this year was new to us. Which is the norm?"

"I don't recall the last time Lem joined us for Christmas. He stays home and has Christmas with his parents." She looked around before leaning forward to whisper, "They drink." She settled back into the red velvet. "So the girls and the grands come here, and Melanie and her brood go back the day after Christmas to have their family holiday then. Claire and Harmony stay a few days longer. Claire likes to be home before New Year's Eve."

"Why did Lem come this year?"

"He didn't really say, just that he was homesick for the old town. He grew up here, but his parents moved to Mississippi when his father inherited the farm there, and he and Melanie followed after their marriage to help out."

I pasted a sympathetic look on my face. "Farming is hard work, as you well know. It's sad that his high school friend died before they had time to reconnect. Did you notice them together?"

"No, I didn't. I was talking with my friends." Her expression shuttered, and her mouth twitched on one side. The three Brandon women had the same generous mouth, with Claire's natural position an easy smile, her mother's prim and ladylike, and Melanie's pinched tight and narrow. Now Miss Leigh looked more like Melanie. "I don't want to speak ill of the dead, but I was relieved to see Melanie and Lem in Mississippi, away from his high school friends, though of course I missed Melanie and the children. No one wanted their children around Guy and Doug, but they could have changed. Doug at least made a tidy fortune, though his soul could be black as an Aberdeen Angus bull. I haven't seen much of Guy. He moved to Austin for a job after high school, and his folks split up and went their separate ways—El Paso and Dallas, I think."

"What kind of trouble?" I asked. When she closed her lips tighter, I added, "What would Mrs. Ly say about them?"

"Oh! You should ask her, but I'm surprised she didn't throw them out, or ask her grandson to. I did hear rumors of drugs, but I don't want to spread gossip when I don't know personally. I know Melanie was relieved to be away from them, but she was never specific, just that it was easier for Lem to be a Christian without them around." She stood and released her lips enough for the slightest of smiles before gliding toward the door. Early deportment and dancing lessons still trumped the onslaught of arthritis. She moved with grace, though slower and more deliberate.

She ushered in Claire before Dianne and I had time for more than a few raised eyebrows in the silent language we've come to call Orchidspeak.

Whereas her mother had perched on the client chair, as the etiquette of her day dictated, Claire, the tallest of her family, leaned back and let it embrace her, definitely not a slouch, just comfortable, so that her smile looked like an invitation.

If you've known me for any length of time, you know I date women my age. Dianne says the standard deviation is plus or minus five, though I can't think of anyone who was five years older, maybe three. On occasion I've been instantly smitten by an older woman—and smite is a good verb for a situation where I feel slapped into another dimension. The first time was when, as a new college freshman, I met Johnny's mother, Solange Vercher. I gawped like a fish and couldn't finish a sentence, all the while my brain screamed, "That's your roommate's *mother*!" As you can imagine, that didn't go anywhere, nor did subsequent mild attractions—there was this poetry teacher.... The most recent time the gong clanged was when I met Claire Brandon last year. That wasn't going anywhere either, with her being my client and all the social difficulties like living across the street from her mother. Claire had to be forty, and I'm aging out of Mrs. Robinson's boy toy category, so maybe the Dustin Hoffman role is not in my future.

She was saying, "It's easier just to do what Mother wants, but I don't see what you could do for me."

Everything the woman did or said seemed like an invitation. I reminded myself that she was a client and Dianne was sitting right next to her. Dianne and I are cool with each other's dating, but not *that* cool. My professional voice sounded a few tones higher to me. "I think it's more of a precaution, so that you'll have counsel in place if you need it. We're trying to establish everyone's background with the victim and his movements today. That will help us determine what might be a conflict of interest."

She looked up to the left, gazing into the past. I tried not to read anything into her fading smile. No one's past is happy, least of all that black hole called high school that our parents assured us would be the best time of our lives. I'm not suicidal, but that almost did me in.

I knew the barest outline of Claire's past. She'd moved to Colorado after high school graduation, where she went to baking school and became a supplier of cannabis edibles to newly legal medical marijuana dispensaries. She opened her own bakery when recreational use became legal. A widow, she had one daughter, Harmony.

Her voice was huskier than normal. "Melanie's three years older than me, just enough that I was out of her social circle, even if she hadn't wanted me out of it. So I knew who Guy was, but not to speak to, me being a lowly freshman who wouldn't have dared. He had a reputation as a bad boy, with drinking and drugs in the picture. Some girls thought he was poison; some found him dangerously attractive. I moved to Colorado for school right after graduation—I couldn't wait to get out of Beauchamp. I never saw him again until today—again, not to speak to, because why would I? Mother's always brought us to Mrs. Ly's open houses, even as adults, and it's always like Old Home Week for me, with people from my school years flitting through. I don't always speak with them—if I didn't then, why would I now? Then too, I'm now the bad girl, with my cannabis bakery. Some people avoid me; some people want me to be their supplier, so I avoid them. I couldn't believe that my mother ever agreed to try medicinal chocolates—after Daddy's death, that was, and I know she shares them with Johnny—but I am not trying to take over Doug Severn's old role as Dealer of Beauchamp."

"She says they're good for nerves," Dianne volunteered.

A smile flickered across Claire's face. "Nerves. Justification for extra prescription pills in my mother's day, day drinking in my grandmother's day, cocaine tonic in my great-grandmother's day. Well, today I noticed the Three Amigos together, but not when they met up or split up."

The door banged open.

"I'm here now," Melanie announced.

Claire looked over her shoulder in acknowledgement. "I think we're done, unless you have something else to ask me?"

"I wanted to ask about Harmony's father," interjected Dianne. Melanie audibly sniffed.

Claire assumed the proper amount of sadness. "My husband died before Harmony was four. She doesn't remember him."

"So not a part of this story at all?" Dianne continued to type.

"I can't imagine how." Claire's farewell smile took in all of us as she conceded the chair to Melanie.

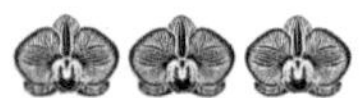

Whereas as Miss Leigh perched on the chair and Claire sank into it, Melanie plopped, indifferent to both its beauty and age. "What did they tell you?" she demanded.

"Client confidentiality means I don't tell you what other clients say, and I don't tell them what you say."

She twisted to face Dianne. "What about you?"

Dianne's eyebrows shot up in shock. "Obviously I understand and practice confidentiality too."

Melanie plopped back into position. "You can't be too careful."

I could disagree with that, but I didn't. "Is there something you're particularly anxious about?"

"I just want to make sure nobody tries to pin this on us, me and my husband, just because we knew Guy in high school."

"Normally police want more evidence than past acquaintance. A court case doesn't even require a motive."

"Well, there isn't a motive. Lem and Guy and Doug loved each other. Like brothers, you understand, like Jonathan and David in the Bible."

I didn't dare look at Dianne, shifting in her velvet chair, the velour of her dress swishing against it. We knew other theories about David and Jonathan from our gay friends.

"Yet he hasn't often returned with you to Beauchamp," I observed. I hadn't thought it possible for her lips to purse any thinner.

"You said this is confidential? Lem had a bad reputation in high school, and sometimes he was led astray by his companions. Then he fell in love with me and found Jesus, but it was hard for him to resist temptation. When his parents inherited the farm in Mississippi and wanted us to join them, I knew it was an answer to prayer, direct from God. We prayed about it and moved after Matthew was born. With his family all around him there, he didn't need to come back to Beauchamp like I did at Christmas. We called that time his 'vacation.' Even happy marriages like ours benefit from time apart. That's in the Bible."

"But this year he wanted to come back?" It's not like I could call God as a witness.

Melanie inched forward, intent on her story. "In the last few years, he's been burdened for their souls. He knew their lives hadn't been as happy as his, because he accepted Jesus. He wanted to urge them to get right with the Lord, and this year he said God was telling him he should come back with me and witness to his friends."

"And did he do that?" I asked.

Melanie scrunched her face up to squeeze back tears. "I don't know. I left them alone, but a party isn't really private, and you heard him say that they were planning to get together later. What if he was going to talk to them then, and now Guy's dead and he'll never hear the Word of God?"

"We'll hope Lem gave them a preview at least, and that was enough to turn Guy's heart. For all we know, maybe he died because he refused to continue his previous way of life." I snuck a glance at Dianne.

She folded her hands and looked out the window in refusal to be part of this prayer meeting. At least she wasn't laughing.

Melanie wiped her eyes. Dianne handed her a tissue from the discreet wooden box on my desk—so discreet that clients usually can't find it. After a good honk, Melanie said, "Thank you, JD. That does bring me comfort. We don't know what miracles God worked in Guy's last minutes."

Since God's actions weren't admissible in a court of law either, I asked, "Do you know when any of them left? Did they leave together? I think Lem was here when the policeman announced the discovery, but I don't think Doug was."

Again with the pinched lips. "Lem went out for a smoke break around three o'clock. He knows it's a sin, and he's working on it. But he went out back alone and came back alone. I don't know what Guy and Doug did." Her tone implied that she didn't care if they went to hell, a contrast from her previous words.

I stood up. "Thank you, Melanie. That's all we need for now. If you want me in your police interview, just tell me."

Dianne stood too. "They're conducting them here at Gregg House."

"And my advice remains the same: Don't offer any information, and answer only the questions I approve."

CHAPTER 7

Wearing our professional smiles, Dianne and I leaned on either side of the door to watch Melanie reunite with the rest of her family. Her mother and sister joined her from the center of the gallery, where the Christmas tree and chairs were, her sons from the back door station, her daughter from the front station.

Pastor Nathan, Miss Leigh's new minister, pressed her hand in sympathy. He hesitated and then did the same to Claire for a second. Their hands flew apart as though burned, but I'm not sure it meant anything other than standard male stupidity, as Dianne says. Niece Harmony remained at the front desk, which now included some Cortez sisters and my sister Cherry, until Claire crooked her finger in a come-here gesture to her daughter.

Melanie's gentle plaint rose above the ambient noise. "Where's Lem?"

As she pushed herself off the desk, Harmony sighed with all the drama of a teenager too old for this stuff. "Every time I miss having a father, I think about Uncle Lem and consider myself lucky."

Cherry matched her sigh. "There's worse things for sure. I used to read books about happy families and wonder where they got these father types. I decided they were fantasy stories, like those about unicorns and aliens."

As Harmony proceeded at molasses speed toward her family, to make it clear her mother wasn't the boss of her, I inserted myself into the group with a grimace of agreement in Cherry's direction. Changing the subject from fathers, I asked, "Did everything go okay with Grandfather? I thought you might feel more comfortable talking to him than me, Cherry."

Her expression would have done credit to a major tragic role, if eye rolls are allowed in Shakespeare. "Oh sure, JD, I totally wanted to explain sexual harassment to someone who had to lick a stamp to post on social media."

Tima Cortez said, earnest, "I appreciated his help. We have an obligation to help our elders understand modern life. I'm glad he's coming into our interviews. He has such an imposing presence."

"I'll come to yours instead if you want, Cherry," I offered. "And Grandfather knows what sexual harassment is; it just wasn't called that or considered wrong."

Cherry shot back, "Not by the menz, it wasn't. You ought to talk to Grandmother. And I want you both with me. There's no point in having a family of lawyers if you can't throw them around to make an impression. They'll both come with you too," she told Dianne's sisters.

"Happy to do it, but who gets which or how many lawyers will depend on the police schedule." I scanned the room. With the Brandon contingent moving toward the back door, I could see that the party was over. With each broken gingerbread house bagged and tagged on the display tables, the atmosphere looked more bereft than your average party's end, though with our families still around, we had enough people for at least a small reception.

Darryl danced in from the clinic and waved a cheery farewell to the Brandons. In his opposite hand, he carried a blue satin cat carrier, bedazzled to the max. I wondered where it came from. It wasn't one of our carriers.

Sophie Thi approached, shoulders hunched. She muttered an apology to the sisters, her eyes darting towards Dianne, who stepped in closer. The apology accepted, conversation turned to self-defense for the Modern Girl and their preferred weapons. It made me sad, remembering how my sisters used to talk about toys, then about boys, clothes, and makeup. Now weaponry?

To redirect my thoughts, I went to help the elves, still scurrying around, doing things with trays of food. I couldn't tell that we had any less than when we started. The remains would appear at church Sunday schools, civic gatherings, and break rooms of local businesses, but we wouldn't start delivering until Sunday morning. Even the sugary scent hung heavy and mournful in the air. Johnny was making an early start on the sixteen tons of frosting we'd need for repairs.

Darryl pranced down the gallery toward us, holding up his phone. "Think I'm ready to record. Can one of you hold the phone? I'm gonna put up a TikTok about Godzilla kitty, to find his people. Johnny says somebody's got to be looking for him, him being such a valuable cat."

"Do people go on TikTok to look for lost cats?" I asked.

"You don't need a reason to go on TikTok. It's one of those automatic things like breathing. Okay, one more rehearsal. I want this to go viral." He turned on his music, something with more bass and beat than anything else, and handed his phone to Juke Cortez before he sang (and danced):

"*Little nakey cat, nakey cat, so squealy*
Little nakey cat, and he's so appealing
Little nakey cat, nakey cat, is he yours? Whose is he?"

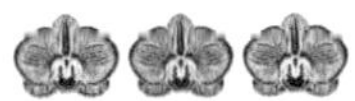

I'm not sure I got all the words, but that was the gist, and the younger crowd—it hurts to type that—thought it was great.

Cherry, who's majoring in arts management, advised, "You need more of Godzilla. Anything with cats sells."

"I got lotsa reels of him. Took some in the clinic, but that looked too institutional, so I brought him in here—around the Christmas tree, in the kitchen—for a few clips. He's there now, in his carrier. You should see it— looks like he's ready for RuPaul, that fabulous, all blinged out with jewels to match his eyes. He must be from a rich family. I had to wrap him in a beach towel, the fierce li'l bugger. Someone must have left him on the clinic porch in his beautified carrier, and he got out, looking for his home, I suspect."

Johnny's grandmother pushed her rolling walker over to Dianne, who'd remained by my office door. As far as I can tell, Mrs. Ly uses assistive devices to look like a decrepit old lady instead of the senior dynamo who walks three miles each day and manages her family and half her acquaintances. She handed Dianne a sparkly Christmas envelope. "Here's the checks and cash people gave me today, Dianne dear."

"I'll put them in the safe," promised Dianne as she flipped through the envelope's contents. "I don't know why people bring money to a party."

Mrs. Ly chuckled. "It's the tradition around here. Those with money want to make sure their neighbors see them being charitable and not mistaken for objects of charity. One thing about Mayor Lorenz, he makes a splashy big donation, and those wanting to curry favor with him follow suit."

"Doug Severn matched the mayor's," noted Dianne, who normally gives confidentiality lessons to oysters, but we were dealing with a murder case. "Guy Randall gave half that, but we won't get it because the bank will freeze his account. I'll try remote deposit, but it's not likely to succeed."

Mrs. Ly's expression went dark and brooding. "Guilt money from those two, but it still spends the same. I don't know why they came back after all these years."

I didn't know whether to look like I understood or whether I didn't; I saw a similar conflict on Dianne's face. Southern manners be damned: this was a murder investigation. "I hope Sophie Thi is doing as well as she seems."

Mrs. Ly sighed. "Sophie Thi came into the world fighting and never stopped, which is how she saved herself. I have to be glad the incident was brief and she had no physical damage that would make a court case. We thought the court process would be grueling for her, as it is for anyone at any age. So we didn't press charges, but I still worry about whether that was the right choice."

I hoped I'd never have to make that kind of decision. I wouldn't want to be involved in such a case, though I hoped some attorney would. As Dianne went to the safe—you don't need to know where that is—I leaned against the wall and let the sounds wash over me.

Merry moved from her door-guarding post to the baby grand piano. She called to Cherry, "JD's got all of our piano music, Cherry. Come play Christmas duets with me." I'd rescued all the piano music after Dad sold the house we grew up in.

Juke and Tima gave advice to Darryl on editing his video, which he didn't always take.

Darryl's voice carried over the twins' inexpert carols, "Johnny says we can't show exactly what Godzilla looks like. He's such a spendy dude, somebody might lie about owning him. He's like a witness protection cat. We'll have to blur his hind end, where that gray spot is, so we can ask people what special markings he has."

"Blur it with sparkles," suggested Juke.

"Ooh, nice!"

Chantal called from the group around Sophie Thi, "Dianne, help! I'm having a shopping crisis. She sells makeup!" Dianne interrupted her return to go talk Chantal out of spending her next month's income on more makeup. What she has might fit in a refrigerator box. It takes up most of her rented room in Austin, her theoretical home.

Underneath the video editing and Beginner's Christmas Duets was the susurrus of young women and a few men from the security detail arguing about where to store the leftover food, with complaints that Johnny had already started not only the icing for house repair but the refreshments for the concert. A few "Kitty, Kitty" coos told me Godzilla was still in the kitchen. Leaning on my grandfather's arm, my grandmother stood near the piano aiming fond smiles at the twins as they clanked through their songs with more cheer than skill.

I realized with a jolt—well, a poke in the arm—that Mrs. Ly was talking to me.

"JD, do you know how long the police will have the crime scene blocked off? They've got the back lot taped off, and that could cause a problem for concert parking. I hate to receive guests with crime scene tape on the premises."

"It depends on how their investigation is going," I replied. "Could be hours, could be days. Al's always reasonable, though. I'll ask him."

Officer Al thundered down the stairs and approached us. "I've a mind to arrest you for obstructing an investigation. How am I supposed to investigate when you've told everybody not to talk to me?"

"It might not be in their best interests to talk to you," I protested.

"How am I going to track anybody's movements?"

"How would you anyway, with half the town swarming here? Look, I'll ask Dianne to send you what info we have about the victim's movements. If we see anything relevant in the squintillion photos taken today, we'll send those too."

"I'm taking all of them as soon as I get a warrant!"

"Too late. Judge Ochoa was here earlier, right at the beginning, and she said she was on her way to the Austin airport for holiday break."

His face was red as the seasonal color. He was about to flame me good when a crash from the kitchen followed by screams sent all of us running that direction. I heard a few clues before we arrived.

"He knocked his carrier over and got out!"

"Get away from him! He's vicious!"

"He ran right through the icing bowl! Look at all the white footprints everywhere!"

"Oh my God! What's he doing?"

I arrived, with Darryl, Juke, and Tima close behind, in time to see for myself. The pink, hairless cat, covered in white puffs, looking like a

Candyland Gollum on a bad hair day, glared at us from his perch in a pan full of rice on the kitchen island. I had maybe three seconds to wonder why he wanted to sit in rice before we heard a stream of liquid squirting on metal.

CHAPTER 8

Mrs. Ly, just now catching up to us, suggested in her quietest tones, "You might want to get that cleaned up before John Ky finds out. It's the kind of thing that would upset him."

The acrid odor wafted through the air, in case anyone was still confused.

"Oh *God*, how could you!" wailed Darryl, confusing those who weren't clear on the cat's name. "Someone's going to die."

"Johnny would never kill a cat," I stated with total certainty.

Hopping around, wringing his hands, Darryl was coming unhinged. "What does that matter when he's gonna kill *me*? I shouldn't have brought Godzilla in here."

Surveying the scene, I assured him, "He won't, but let's mitigate the damage. You—"

Chantal called from the dining room, "Yes, you, Darryl. This is on you. I ain't cleaning no kitchen litter box."

"—need to take the pan outdoors for its first cleaning," I finished.

Darryl took three steps into the kitchen, towards the island. Godzilla sprang into a defensive position, four legs braced in a crouch, ready to spring. He lashed his whip of a tail and growled deep in his throat, just like his big cousins and ancestors. Like my ancestors when confronted with such a beast, I wanted to run. Everyone stepped back.

Never taking his eyes off the livid cat, Darryl whispered to Dianne's brother, "Zap, grab that tablecloth next to you, the one covering the food. You take one end, and I'll take the other. We'll move forward and catch him, like in a big parachute, like we did earlier."

Zap looked doubtful. "You sure? He could rip right through that."

"So get two," whispered Darryl. "We gotta keep him as far from us as possible. Somebody bring in an outdoor trash bin. We'll set him in that after we catch him."

"What you're paying me does not cover cat catching," Zap stated, eyeing Godzilla, now pacing back and forth across his island kingdom.

But he handed Darryl the other end of the festive tablecloth. They spread their arms wide to make a banner of poinsettias and moved forward with small steps. Godzilla snarled, his skin rippling in fury. He crouched even lower. His eyes darted from Zap to Darryl as he decided on his first target.

"You bunch of babies." Chantal pulled the tablecloth away. Zap and Darryl stepped back into the crowd with obvious relief. "He's just a baby cat. Aren't you, sweetums? Just a li'l kitty-kitty, all alone in the world."

She glided forward, her hands at her waist, but spread wide. The diameter of the tail lashing shrank. The yowling sank to a conversational level, his battle cry now a plaintive chant, and the wrinkles in his furious forehead smoothed out.

In the same soft sing-song, her eyes still on Godzilla, Chantal said, "All you idiots, back off, way off. I'm coming through with this kitty, and I don't want you scaring him."

"I'll get his carrier for you," offered Darryl, blanching when he saw how close Chantal stood to it.

"He don't like it, and he don't like y'all. Just you clear out the way. I said, *way* out."

Godzilla leapt into Chantal's arms before she reached the island. As he sank those long claws into her shoulder and cried, she held him close. He rubbed against her cheek and shoulder and transferred icing to her hair, skin, and clothes. I raised my eyebrows in astonishment as I waved everybody back.

"You got you some sharp razors on those feet, sweetie. Let's go someplace else. These folks be cray. You don't have to dance for no Tik-Tok. I know you don't like the clinic, but it's better than here, right?"

When I stepped backwards, I landed on Officer Al's foot and stumbled into Cupcake. That might have led to words—or Cupcake's ripping my throat out—but Johnny's voice cut through, quiet as always, but compelling. "Do as Chantal says. Give her space and quiet to get the cat to safety."

People shuffled around, revealing Johnny by the clinic door. They left Chantal a wide path that she glided through like a queen, head held high. Godzilla scowling over her shoulder at us peasants reinforced the royal vibe. Johnny opened the door for the woman-and-cat procession and then backed away to let them through. Godzilla hissed at him.

After he shut the door behind them, he retrieved the ridiculous cat carrier and held it out to Officer Al. "I think someone left the cat in this carrier on my clinic porch. The cat then got out and proceeded to the front porch, where we found him swinging on the hanging flower baskets. I found the carrier later and photographed it before bringing it in to check for fingerprints and DNA. My intern didn't understand that it might be evidence and used it to bring the cat in here, but you still might want to check it, though I'll provide my results to you. I put out some evidence flags on the porch and in the path. I've already taken photographs. The security camera footage doesn't show a person—as though the person knew there was a camera and stayed out of its range—but I'll study it more closely this evening."

"I can't believe this!" Officer Al exploded.

Cupcake pricked up her ears, ready to defend at the slightest excuse or command. I sidled away, which would be useless if she decided I was the problem.

"I'll share the footage with you," Johnny assured him. "The cat does have a microchip, but in one of those mishaps we see too often, neither the issuing organization nor the owner recorded it. On Monday I should be able to track the clinic or shelter that received the chip, and they'll probably remember this cat. He's quite unusual and very valuable. Maybe by then we'll see someone searching for him."

"I made a TikTok to post," offered Darryl.

"Thank you, Darryl. You may do so right after you clean the kitchen."

Darryl made a show of taking the litter box-rice pan outdoors.

Officer Al shouted, "What's with you people? Do you think I'm investigating a cat napping? There was a murder in your backyard. Remember?"

"That reminds me," I said with a nod to Mrs. Ly. "Do you expect to release the scene by Monday? We're hosting a concert, and we'd rather not have to do it while wrapped in crime scene tape."

"Concert! Cat carrier! You're lucky I don't wrap the whole property in crime scene tape." As Cupcake growled her agreement, Al patted her head. "There now, girl, it's okay."

"If you did, then you'd want to look at the clinic porch," said Johnny with insufferable logic. "And we'd have to move out until you release the scene. Our party assistants are staying the night, so we'd need—how many beds, Dianne?"

"Twenty-four," she announced, grim as a traffic ticket. "That's your family, JD's, and mine."

All out of answers, at least ones that he wanted witnessed, Al growled along with his dog and said, "Come on, Cupcake."

The crowd fell back like the Red Sea. No one had to be told to give them space. Cupcake was famous. Officer Al stomped out the back door, with Cupcake prancing and grinning by his side, to let us know there were no hard feelings and did we have any treats to spare?

Conversations erupted as soon as he slammed the door shut, most of them around getting to the traditional after-open house for dinner and drinks, many drinks, at Casa Gracias, all on Black Orchid Enterprises' tab. Dianne winced in anticipation of the bill.

"Everybody's walking," declared Darryl. Downtown Beauchamp is just a few blocks away from Gregg House. "Well, not you, Mrs. Ly. Or Mrs. Cortez. Or JD's grandparents. The rest of you can take off your spikes and put on your walking shoes. Everybody take a different path and put up Found Cat posters for Godzilla on the way. Maybe you people who're driving could put a few in the businesses on the highway."

Johnny sighed in sorrow and stared at the ground. "I thought he'd want to investigate any unusual activity on the premises around the same time as the murder."

Always fair, Dianne said, "But is someone abandoning a cat on our porch even unusual?"

"Usually they ring the bell and give a sob story," I argued.

"But what about that time—"

Johnny cut in. "I think I'll stay home tonight. I must finish making the icing and start the concert refreshments again. And I need to go through all the photos." He looked wan.

Dianne raised her voice and silenced the room. "All of you uploaded your photos to our cloud, right? I want you to look through them and tag any photos of the murder victim and his friends. Just mark them as favorite."

"And tag anything that looks odd," I added, wondering what kind of can of worms that would open. It's an odd house, to say the least.

"And any photos that include the back door, back porch, clinic, or back yard," Johnny decreed.

"Do it before you have your first drink." I interrupted his list. I didn't want every photo taken today to be tagged.

Returning from the back yard, Darryl bowed low in front of Johnny to present the shiny, clean rice pan. Johnny returned to the kitchen, its island still covered in white icing paw prints and globs.

I murmured to Dianne, "You know Johnny's going to sit up all night anyway looking at every photo, right? Or he would if he were investigating this crime."

"I can't tell if he is, though he's on the trail of that cat's owner."

Dianne ran her hand through her hair, which made it look even better. Women hate her. One of my dating tests is to see whether meeting my old friend and partner makes them dissolve into jealous green goo. "At least we'll have some photos to send to Al, which might calm him down. We can't afford to stay on his bad side."

I agreed. "Be nice if we could hand him the murderer too. At least point him in the right direction."

Dianne glanced around before moving closer to whisper to me. The madding crowds were streaming towards the exits in their quest for enchiladas and margaritas. Everyone carried a handful of Found Cat fliers, fluttering like a swarm of cat-patterned butterflies.

"It's obvious to me. Lem did it. He and his 'friends' show up after twenty years, and one of them is murdered."

I whispered in her ear, "I hear those air quotes."

"Didn't you see those men, Doug, Guy, and Lem? They weren't good buddies glad to see each other. They kept throwing insults, the kind that are supposed to be funny, but aren't. You could have cut the tension with a butter knife."

"You noticed all that?"

"They were the kind of guys you keep your eye on."

"So I've heard. Are your sisters okay? Cherry seemed to shrug off his 'advances.'"

"We've all been working Mami's parties since we were toddlers. We can take care of ourselves, but it's annoying, and definitely raises red flags: What else might those guys have the nerve to do?"

"I agree, but Officer Al needs some real evidence." I held up my hands to hold back the attack warned by her flashing eyes. "Courtroom evidence, I mean. I vote for Lem too. Can you imagine turning down a free attorney?"

Dianne nodded, appeased. "He's got secrets, and I bet one of them is that he murdered Guy Randall. We just need to find out why."

"Nope. That's a police job, and they actually don't have to prove a motive in court. We don't have any hard evidence for Al, but maybe the photos will show something. There's no rush—Lem's a prisoner at Miss Leigh's house for Christmas."

As Chantal emerged from the clinic into the gallery, raising its population to three, I asked, "Did you save Chantal from another makeup binge?" I was thinking I could buy her Christmas present from Sophie Thi's supply.

"Yes. Sophie Thi gave us a two-for-one discount, so we both got starter kits. I paid for them, and I'll take Chantal's share out of what we pay her for income tax work. She needs all her party fees for the holidays. You wouldn't believe this makeup. It's actually made for—and by—people of color, instead of white folks' makeup colored dark."

"That's great," I said, declining comment on any part of her statement. It wouldn't end well.

Chantal whispered, "I sang him to sleep and tiptoed out."

Dianne looked around, seeing no one else in the cavernous hall. "Johnny?"

"No, stupid. Godzilla. Johnny's in the clinic looking after the other cats, but Godzilla hates him. First time ever a cat didn't like Johnny. Hope he can take it. JD, can you turn the Kitty Cam on remote so I can keep an eye on Zil from the restaurant?" She dropped her voice low. "I'd stay here, but this is the perfect opportunity to practice Johnny's song in full voice, in public."

Our group present for Johnny was to sing a Jewish song for him at Monday night's concert. Chantal discovered it, a three-part harmony evening prayer, and we agreed that Johnny might like that, what with the Judaism studies he began this past year. Chantal snatched every opportunity away from Johnny for rehearsal, and this one was perfect.

We'd have an audience, and there was no danger of Johnny walking in. MultiABBA, with varying personnel, often spontaneously sings karaoke style in Casa Gracias. The management must like it; they keep comping our food. Not drinks, though, and not for everybody we bring in with us.

Dianne agreed, while keeping an eye on the clinic door. "Normally I'd try to talk Johnny into going, at least for a few minutes, but as you say, it's the perfect opportunity to practice his song. Lots of Anglos go to Casa

Gracias on Saturday night. They'll just think we're singing in Spanish, and Latinos will think we've got bad accents."

"All true," I said. "Though they ought to know better about you. It's been a long, tough day. Let's just kick back tonight before we do Infrastructure Day on the gingerbread town and get ready for the concert. Tomorrow's bound to be easier."

CHAPTER 9

I was wrong. I wanted to sleep until Wednesday, because we and our guests had literally staggered home—since we'd walked there, posting flyers as we went—at closing time after consuming equal numbers of tacos, enchiladas, and margaritas, some of which we exchanged for drunken musical performances. Everyone sang along, except for Johnny's song. Nobody noticed it was in Hebrew, but everybody cried, it was so beautiful. I took that with a gallon of margarita salt. Most things sound beautiful with alcohol added.

We danced too, and I'll always treasure the vision of my grandfather doing a foxtrot with Johnny's grandmother, a restrained, Anglified salsa with Dianne's mother—and a delicate waltz with my grandmother, cutting quite a rug, as he'd say. Casa Gracias' music system not having an approximation of a waltz, MultiABBA obliged with ABBA's "Move On." I'm glad Merry captured both the dance and the music on her phone.

My phone shrieked in emergency mode at 7:00 A.M. the next day.

I mumbled into it while someone on the other end screamed into my ear until I said "Wrong number" and hung up. Then someone and their army started cosplaying the Battle of the Alamo at our front door. I checked to make sure no body parts were hanging out of my clothes before I stumbled downstairs. The Spanish cursing behind me on my right and utter silence on my left told me Dianne and Johnny were close behind.

I opened the door to a contingent from Miss Leigh's house. A grim-faced Claire Brandon led the posse of her mother supporting Melanie, sobbing like a banshee. No getting out of it, I had to step back and invite them in, despite the Spanish diatribe Dianne hissed in my ear. My mother raised me right. Thanks a lot, Mom. It's not like you're putting up with crazy neighbors at obscene hours of the morning.

By the time I led them back to the kitchen, Johnny's grandmother had creaked out of bed and joined us.

I slapped the coffee pot into action and asked what was wrong.

All three Brandons spoke at once. I took the first cup of coffee for myself. There was a delay while everyone gave me their orders: black for Miss Leigh, with butter for Claire, with three sugars, double cream for Melanie, who then announced that her husband didn't come home all night. They had a fight when she got home, and he said she was making him sick. He then went out and never came back. What should she do? Call the police?

I exchanged looks with Dianne and Johnny, and they slithered towards the back door, just like they were going on their normal morning walk. I suppressed a sigh and mixed pancake batter, like I do most mornings, while encouraging Melanie to tell me all about it.

When I spied an opening in the sobs, recriminations, and awfulizing, I asked in my most casual voice, as though it didn't matter at all, "Had he talked to the police?"

"Yes, he said that was my fault too. But I didn't tell them where he was!"

"Wouldn't have been hard to figure out," I said. "They wanted to talk to everyone who was here yesterday. It wasn't like they singled him out."

"He thought they did, because Guy was his friend. I was so glad we moved away, away from those horrible men."

I spotted Dianne at the back door, gesturing to me. I left Melanie to her family and the other women in the kitchen. I retrieved a no-sugar Pepsi from the refrigerator and brought it to Dianne on the back porch.

She sank onto the wicker sofa with a sigh as she popped the top. I thought she was going to drink the whole thing in one swig, but finally she set it down on the end table.

"Lem's dead. Johnny's staying with him until the police get there. He's lying on the sidewalk on Austin Drive between Alabama and Georgia Streets, a few blocks away."

I stood up again. "I'd better join him."

"Yeah, you're his emotional support lawyer." Dianne took another gulp before rising. "I'll go with you."

"Why?"

"Because I'm not going in the house, that's why. It's Officer Alejandro's job to give people bad news."

"That's why he gets the big bucks," I agreed. "Besides, he's trained in it. How did Lem die?"

"I couldn't tell, and Johnny wasn't speculating. There wasn't any blood, and the corpse was still Lem-shaped. It looked like he just fell over dead. Johnny can't examine the body yet; he needs his crime scene kit. We can go in the clinic entrance to get it from his office. We should grab his jacket too, more if he's got them. The temperature's dropped twenty degrees since yesterday."

"No kidding!" I shivered, hoping Johnny had an extra coat in his office. I wasn't going back in the house either.

The clinic cats told us they hadn't eaten for a week, but I knew better. Dianne looked for jackets while I retrieved the crime scene kit from the office closet. I opened it for a quick check but slammed it shut and scooted when the adjoining door rattled.

We made it out the clinic door with Darryl's voice behind us, saying that he had fed the cats already; he didn't know why they were yelling.

Dianne squeezed herself into the only other coat. Being Darryl's, it fit neither of us, but she at least could get her arms through the sleeves.

The sky looked ready to throw a full-blown winter tantrum, but this being Texas, I didn't take it seriously. We jogged for warmth, not because we were anxious to get there. I've seen more dead bodies this last year than in my whole life. I try to position myself close enough to hear conversations but far enough away to avoid seeing details.

Dianne hung back at the corner of Austin and Alabama, where she wrapped her arms around herself as she shivered. I planned to rejoin her after I checked in with Johnny, who was using his phone to photograph the body and the surroundings, mostly vacant lots, and bemoaning the lack of his good camera. Lem did look like he'd decided to sleep on the sidewalk. Had he lain here all night?

"What do you think?" I asked, looking up for a better line of sight as I handed him his kit and coat. "Yeah, I know you have to wait for the autopsy. Think you'll have trouble getting the officials to agree? Maybe he had some kind of underlying condition just waiting to explode."

Johnny handed me his phone to hold while he shrugged into his puffy coat. "Maybe, but I doubt it would produce the drop of blood by the tear in his sweater."

CHAPTER 10

I squinted at the photo and then the sweater—not the slack, dead face. I'd have to assume there was a hole, also a drop of anything on the dark green, because I didn't want to get up close and personal with a corpse.

Johnny greeted his crime scene kit like it was a brandy barrel on a St. Bernard's neck. Brandy sounded good, with the cold, threatening sky and me in the sweatshirt that's sufficient for all but five days of Texas winter.

I raked my gaze over and away from the body. It's worse when you knew the corpse as a person. Lem had four teenage children and a wife. They would flail around the Lem-shaped hole in their lives for years, maybe forever. I know; my mother died when I was nineteen.

Etched in their memories would be the Christmas sweater that he wore from yesterday's party, probably a gift. You wouldn't buy it for yourself.

A police car disgorged Officer Al and Cupcake, ears flopping in opposite directions. Tongue out, eyes rolling, she looked happy to see us, a source of treats for good dogs.

Our former friend shouted, "You couldn't even give me time to go to Mass this morning."

Johnny pulled on his crime scene booties. "The Cortez family says there are more services later, including one in Spanish at two o'clock."

"And I will be working the crime scene for all of them," Officer Al snarled.

Confused, Cupcake looked up to her owner and then at us. She thought we were the good guys. Still, her officer knew best. She fluffed her ruff in solidarity, morphing from goofy, friendly pup to killing machine, awaiting orders. I kept an eye on her.

Johnny pulled on his gloves. "He's Mrs. Brandon's son-in-law and JD's client."

The officer's face flamed. "Another client? Another 'conflict of interest?'"

Cupcake went from demented to lethal as Officer Al's voice rose.

I froze. I've seen Cupcake take down a perpetrator.

Dianne pulled out her little purse. I swallowed hard as I remembered yesterday's conversation about self-defense precautions. My sister preferred keychain mace; Dianne's cousin liked splayed keys; Sophie Thi sheathed a small knife in her boot. Dianne still carries the little .22 handgun she's had since freshman year. Back then, she opened her purse and told me she didn't need me or anybody else to protect her. I said the same thing now that I said then, at the same volume, "Jeez, Dianne!"

Everyone, including Cupcake, looked at me, puzzled. Dianne waved a dismissive hand and jogged down Alabama Street towards downtown. I didn't know what she was doing, but I heaved a sigh of relief that she didn't draw a gun on a police officer. That could not end well.

I tried my soothing voice. "Officer, you don't want Johnny to testify about his relationships with people involved in the case."

"JD!" Johnny jumped to his feet.

"Tell me about these relationships, JD." An evil smile spread over the policeman's face as he looked from Johnny to me. Cupcake pulled back her lip, mirroring him.

I edged away, eyes on the dog's teeth. "That's privileged communication. How about we send curated photos from yesterday?"

"All!" growled the officer, echoed by his dog.

"When we see the warrant. Would you call off Cupcake?" My stomach clenched as she moved closer. When Cupcake takes down perps, they need medical treatment before the police can question them.

"She won't do that unless I say—"

"Don't say it!" Johnny and I both exclaimed.

The officer sighed. "The command. She won't do anything until I give the command. How dumb do you think I am?"

The husky rolled her blue eye in my direction. I worried that she might go freelance.

Johnny offered, "You can have all the photos."

"Not those of my clients!" I objected.

"Then *you* upload them after examining them." The razor-thin edge in Johnny's voice made clear his opinion of people who spent their nights dining, drinking, dancing, and sleeping instead of studying case photos.

Officer Al grinned in pleasure at our quarrel.

Shuddering at my day's task, I glanced at Cupcake's owner. "Your upload site better have enough space for the Library of Congress." To the officer's appalled expression, I explained, "Twenty-something twenty-somethings of the selfie generation took photos all afternoon."

Johnny tapped his phone, probably texting the medical examiner. "He needs an autopsy. There's a stab wound on his chest from a thin, narrow blade."

"How can a wound as small as a mosquito bite cause death?" argued Officer Al.

Cupcake growled again. I looked in vain for a defensive weapon. The block was littered, but not with anything useful.

No one saw Dianne's return. I smelled the steaming bags she carried first.

She smiled. "Here's donuts and coffee from Ming's."

I reached into a bag and stripped the breading from a kolache. "Can I give this to Cupcake so she won't rip my arm off?"

"She will, if I say—"

"Don't say it!" exclaimed Dianne.

"How stupid do you think he is, Dianne?" I asked.

Officer Al frowned. "I don't like other people feeding her."

As exaggerated as a royal equerry, I handed him the half-bare sausage. "Cupcake, observe that I give this sausage for distribution to you only."

Her eyes and ears lined up. Officer Al held out his hand, and the sausage vanished. I tried not to imagine what she could do to fingers in the same instant.

Johnny's voice soothed like heavy cream in the bitter coffee. "Officer Al, I know you love Cupcake. She's confused and under stress, thinking she might have to attack any minute, especially people she knows. You're free to hold a grudge until our fourth-level descendants offer prayers for us, but please don't keep your dog in this misery."

Officer Al stooped down and murmured to Cupcake until she relaxed and panted in our general direction. After a few gulps of courage, hot and sweet, he went to inform the family.

Leaving Johnny to work the crime scene with the police, which looked like the most boring one ever, if you didn't count the body, Dianne and I strolled back home, slower this time, being full of donuts and coffee.

Dianne's breath puffed into little clouds. "You did notice that we're rotten detectives, right? Our chief suspect is dead."

I considered for a few more puffs. "Maybe somebody killed him because he killed Guy."

"Are you attached to that idea?"

"No. Bad thing, getting attached to ideas." I hoped our next ones were better.

We didn't enter Gregg House until after the Brandon family dragged themselves back across the street. Our guests were breakfasting on left-over pastries in the kitchen-dining area. They gave a few obligatory gasps at the news, but the younger Cortezes were bent on convincing Mamí/Tía Conchita that the weather was too bad to venture out; they hadn't brought warm clothes. Mrs. Cortez decreed that Dianne should empty her closet for them. To Dianne's response of "How many winter outfits do you think I have?" Mrs. Cortez proclaimed that they'd be fine once they were inside the church, only a five-minute drive away. Father Emilio would be disappointed not to see them.

Mrs. Cortez has more of a relationship with the local priest than Dianne does. She trudges to Mass once a month in hopes that he won't report her to her mother.

The young people vanquished, they clumped up the stairs to get ready. Cherry and Sophie Thi gathered plates of treats to take to the churches. Merry claimed a severe headache, a product of sudden weather changes.

The ancestral contingent paced off the gallery, planning the concert seating and protocol, leaving me and Merry, peeling a grapefruit into segments. She looked so miserable that I got up to make her another cup of hot tea, some herbal mess that smelled like orange.

We Thompson kids look similar: tall, with curly blonde hair and bright blue eyes. I like to think I rock a masculine version, and Cherry spends a lot of time straightening her curls and cutting them into angles, but Merry's always been a softer version, downright angelic at times, tender and sweet—a dead ringer for the Virgin Mary, if you think the Middle Eastern teenager who bore Jesus had curly blonde hair and blue eyes, like all the imaginary portraits in every church I've attended.

By the time I brought the tea to her, she'd gobbled the fruit. Rio Grande grapefruits are that juicy and sweet. Her hand now hovered first over a donut, then a kolache, then an eclair, and back to the donut, before grabbing a brownie from another plate and tearing into it like a starving coyote.

"Big Tex has the best brownies," she informed me in defensive tones. "We don't have a Big Tex in Waco, not close."

"So I've heard." I pushed the bowls of sweetener and lemon to her.

She doctored her tea with the same ferocious attention she'd give a lab experiment. "I screwed up, didn't I?"

"I'm not aware of it, though we all do sometimes."

She took a first sip of tea and winced at the heat. She set the mug down with a thump. "The murderer had to walk by me yesterday, and I didn't see him."

"Or her. If they'd worn a name tag saying, 'Hi, I'm the Murderer,' you would have noticed that. We didn't hire you as security."

"Good thing, since I was so rotten at it. I stayed there all afternoon, except for when I went to the bathroom. A Cortez cousin would cover for me then, but they didn't see anything either."

"Merry, we hired you to get people to sign our guest book and take photos of those guests."

She tested the tea again and could now take a few sips. "I took a photo of everybody who would let me. Doug Severn didn't want me to. He was pretty rude about it, so I snapped him from behind when he was talking to his friends, just to get even. Also when he went out in the backyard on his way out and tossed the football with the Cortez cousins for a while."

"Then you did your job. We did hire the Cortez cousins as security, as well as backup for you, but they were protecting the cat shelter, not investigating a murder. I'm sure they did their job too. The cats are safe."

Chantal staggered in from the clinic and flopped at the table. "He's doing fine. He ate out of my hand."

Just like that, Godzilla had become the only cat in the world to her.

She swiped her phone over the blood sugar monitor on her arm before rummaging through the food for something suitable for a diabetic.

"There's a can of peanuts in the pantry," I offered.

"There better be a kolache in here somewhere."

Merry pushed a plate toward her. Chantal ripped off the bread and popped the sausage in her mouth, reminding me of Cupcake. I handed her a cup of coffee to wash it down.

"So why are you guys lounging around the table on Infrastructure Day? We got a town to rebuild."

I foresaw mountains of white icing in my immediate future. But something else took precedence. "Chantal, you know those reels and photos Darryl sent you yesterday? If Merry doesn't mind, I'd like you to Photoshop a shot of her and Godzilla into the Virgin Mary and Demon Child, all icon-like, with gold leaf background."

"You think the Virgin Mary was blond?"

"It's a deeply held tenet of white Christianity."

"Huh. Not in my church. You don't think this is sacrilegious?"

"It's for Dianne's Christmas present."

"Oh. She'll love it. Just don't let Mrs. Cortez see it."

Mrs. Cortez' devotion led her to name her children after Marian shrines (Guadalupe Dianne, Lourdes, Zapopan, Fatima, and Juquila Candelaria), and my project was not for her eyes. Dianne would think it hysterical. Merry didn't mind being immortalized that way. Chantal promised to get right on it, after Infrastructure Day.

CHAPTER 11

Setup would have gone faster except for the people dropping by to pick up treats for their Sunday schools. I didn't know Beauchamp had that many churches, but it's Texas, so maybe so. Maybe some got a double helping from Cherry and Sophie Thi's deliveries. That bothered me not at all.

Also, people stopped by to see Godzilla—not possible owners, just people on their way to restaurants or other places of worship who wanted to see the weird cat.

Then there was the dryer lint lady, a sweet-faced woman of middle age and middle size who looked perfectly normal, not at all like she sat around all day making portraits of cats from dryer lint.

"I was at Casa Gracias last night and saw your flyer—and heard Darryl sing his song—and Dianne said I could come by this morning to see this cat."

Chantal was off doing something, so I put on a frozen smile to go with the weather. I texted Dianne in the hinterlands of her bedroom as another even more normal-looking woman mounted the steps behind the lint artist.

Dianne: Yes, I did. She's the lady who takes our dryer lint. For art.

JD: Dryer lint?!?!?!?!

Dianne: Anything can be art. Aren't you the bass trombetta squash player in the Beauchamp All-Vegetable Orchestra?

JD: Cat portraits in dryer lint?

Dianne: Just let her see the cat. Lourdes is trying to steal my cashmere sweater, and she'll stretch it out.

That left me with nothing to do but guide the visitors back to the clinic, where I found Chantal sweet-talking Godzilla in his cage. When he saw us, he howled and threw himself at the bars, his limbs splaying in every direction.

"He is—interesting," said the Dryer Lint Lady. "I wonder how I can represent a furless cat—he really is furless, isn't he?—with dryer lint, which has so much cat fur from cat households."

"Totally naked," I agreed.

The second woman, taller, slimmer, and richer, if her coat and boots were any indication, made a noise in her throat. It might have been speech, but I couldn't tell with Godzilla screaming. She shut the clinic door behind her and leaned against it, as far from the cage as possible. I wouldn't have gone nearer the raging beast either.

The artist held up her phone and frowned as she moved around the room, searching for a good angle, one that didn't have an extended limb, claws out, and a view of cat fangs. "I wanted to get a good photo of him to work from."

"Don't think he's feeling photogenic," said Chantal. "Maybe he don't like being a star. Lotta people came to see him this morning, and he's done with all that."

"Darryl took some good shots of him yesterday. I'll ask him to send you some," I offered.

"Thank you." She tapped her contact info to me. "His flyer was so cute. As long as I'm here, I might as well clean your lint catcher."

"You can check out our TikTok too," Chantal suggested. "Darryl posted his song there, with some reels of Godzilla."

"Oh, TikTok, sure. I can freeze frame and do a screen cap."

I looked at her in some doubt. The generation before me isn't supposed to be so tech hip. "Some of him is blurred out, for witness protection, Darryl says."

She waved an unconcerned hand. "I can cope. Or just wait for the photos. Lint felting isn't a rapid process."

We filed back into the house, and I directed her to the basement stairs, where the dryer lived.

"I know my way," she said cheerily as she clopped down the stairs.

"What will happen to the cat?" asked the other woman as she pulled her patterned wool scarf tighter around her neck. "This is a shelter, isn't it?"

"Also known as the Cat Copacabana, premier resort for discriminating felines."

Her lips disappeared as she gripped them together, despite all the lipstick. "You're not going to put him to sleep, are you?"

"My partner will evict all his roommates to make room for more cats before he'd put one to sleep. Come to think of it, I already sleep with multiple cats. We still have hopes of finding Godzilla's owner, but if that doesn't pan out, and no one wants to adopt him, he'll have a home here." I swallowed hard at the thought of daily Godzilla vs. the Very Good Kitties struggles. "I'm not sure that's a workable business model in the long run, but that's how things work for now. He'll have a good home, one way or another."

"Thank you." She turned and swept out the way she came in, followed shortly by the dryer lint lady, rejoicing at her new bags of prey.

By the time the warmly beglamoured Cortez contingent came down the stairs, Chantal had the workstations organized at both the food tables and gingerbread display tables. The endless decorations—the massive Christmas tree, bedazzled green wreaths and sprays, candles and lights on any surface that would hold them—and our cheery construction supplies gave the place a weird vibe, like a North Pole sweatshop. Instead of sweat and grime, the place smelled like sugary icing, fresh baked gingerbread, and candy. I wondered if Santa's workshop was unionized and whether they needed legal representation.

The dozen or so Cortez sisters and cousins cooed and lied about how sorry they were to leave us behind. I thought about lobbing a candy cane at Dianne's smirk, but decided I must be more mature than that. Or I should pretend to be.

With Darryl still caring for the shelter and clinic cats—except for Godzilla, whom he left for Chantal—the workforce was reduced to my grandparents, Mrs. Ly, Merry, and me. Chantal was more of a supervisor and purveyor of supplies, tools, original photographs, and advice. She gave me the houses in the worst condition, because I had the most construction experience.

I grimaced at the pile of crumbs and candy shards as I reflected on the longevity of some mistakes. Back in our sophomore college year, after we moved into a decrepit old mansion near the University of Texas campus, I inflated my home repair skills in an effort to impress my roommates—okay, Dianne. My only credentials were working on a Habitat for Humanity house with my high school church group (I painted ceiling trim, because of my height) and helping fellow Eagle Scout candidates build sheds. I'd no idea the country had such a demand for sheds, the standard Eagle project. Everyone was thrilled with my project because they could just give me money for my popup and online back-to-school store for a disadvantaged neighborhood school.

That slight exaggeration led me to many new skills and today's assignment. I cut gingerbread slices into load-bearing walls (while the others pasted icing on cracks and covered damage with bits of candy) when Johnny returned from the newest crime scene.

"Problems?" I asked as I measured my walls and their angles.

"No. The police didn't quarrel with the need for an autopsy, and my job ended when I arranged for that. I explained to them that Lem was married to our client, so I thought there could be another conflict of interest. Officer Al was angry, but they wanted to be done quickly, with the weather getting so bad. A winter storm is expected."

The view out the row of windows lining the back of the house confirmed the threat, though it looked more like the troops in the sky gathering to attack, with no actual thunder or precipitation yet. Being Texas, we might get cold rain.

Chantal broke up our conference. "Johnny, come look at Godzilla. He was upset with all the people coming to look at him this morning. He's still got icing on him from yesterday, too. I tried to wipe him off, but he didn't want me to, and I missed some, and now it's caked on."

Johnny snapped into his favorite subject. "Sphynx cats need to be bathed regularly. I noticed yesterday he needed a bath, even without the icing. And they need to be oiled so their skin doesn't dry out. Darryl, help me bathe Godzilla."

Still in his cat tending clothes, a shabby set of sweats that had started life as brown and disintegrated into something unnameable, Darryl stood at the back door, just coming in from tending the shelter cats in the converted barn. He looked from the gingerbread house chain gang to the clinic door and sighed in the direction of neither. He trudged after Johnny to the clinic. Overtime doesn't make up for everything.

I had all the walls of my miniature castle shored up—why did it have to be a castle?—and was considering the roof when the screams started. I raised my head and looked at my fellow builders, also puzzled.

Chantal frowned as she lifted her gaze from her lavender candy house shingles. "They better not be hurting that cat."

She was marching toward the clinic when the door flew open. Johnny stumbled out, supporting Darryl, covered in blood and limping on a bloody leg.

"That cat bit me!" he moaned. "First my arm, all up and down. Then he jumped down and chawed on my leg. Thought he was gonna take it off."

Over the gasps of horror, Johnny shouted as he kicked the door shut behind him. "I have to take Darryl to the emergency room. Don't go in the clinic. We had to leave Godzilla running loose, but he can't hurt himself."

"The poor kitty! You scared him!" cried Chantal. But she didn't go into the clinic.

Darryl scowled at her over his shoulder as Johnny pulled him out the door, a move that left the door frame bloody.

A shocked pall hung over the room, which always has a hushed vibe, thanks to the tall ceilings and heavy old furniture. Merry's lip trembled. Mrs. Ly continued to count peppermint sticks as she remarked, "You'll want to clean up the blood before it sets."

Chantal and I eyed the trail of blood from clinic to back door and the blood smears on both doors.

She threw up her hands. "You hired me to put on your blasted party, two of them in fact, plus organize a concert, not clean up a crime scene. Your house, you clean it."

"This was not covered in law school," I muttered as I headed for the cleaning supplies.

I started with the doors because they were a lighter color than the wood floors. Merry helped. She watched and called out, "You missed a spot." Constantly. As I was wiping down the back door, Officer Al arrived and almost got his face wiped.

He took a step back and exclaimed, "Not another one!"

"Not a murder, just an attempted one, and we have the perp contained." I looked around for Chantal, who would surely protest. "The new cat bit Darryl, and Johnny took him to the emergency room. Darryl, not the cat."

Officer Al huffed. "I hope you're going to put him down. He's dangerous."

"Darryl? He's harmless. And the cat was scared, doing what scared cats do. But their long, skinny fangs go so deep that it's easy to get an infection from a bite. Before we hired Darryl, I made several trips to the ER with cat bites. Occupational hazard."

"Johnny was going to send me photos from yesterday."

I took him to my office and hauled out my laptop. "Sorry. He's got a file marked for you, but I don't have access to it."

"Dianne was going to send me a timeline of Guy Randall's movements at the open house. I want her to add Lem's as well."

"Dianne's at Mass with her family. She must not be finished with the first file, because I don't have access to that either. She doesn't show her work until it's perfect."

Anger and sorrow warred on his face. Like any reasonable heterosexual man, he adored Dianne, but from afar, like everyone nowadays. Her letting him down was too much to bear. He reached into a pocket and pulled out something in a clear plastic bag that he shoved in my face. "What does that mean to you?"

I blinked. It was an invitation to our open house and concert, with *20 30.02* scribbled on it in blue ballpoint ink that skipped. I tried to figure out what else it might mean, either what I read or what might be concealed in the skips. Possessing the card meant nothing; we distributed those invitations all over town. I gave up. "30.02 is the Texas penal code for burglary."

The policeman snorted.

"Come on, man. I'm a lawyer. What else would I think it is?"

He stuffed it back in his pocket. "Why would Lem Quiston have it in his pocket?"

I kept my face blank. "That's not what we talked about. I've no idea what it meant to him. I told you what it means to me."

"And I suppose you can't tell me a thing about this latest murder because he was your client, as well as his wife and her whole family."

"That's right," I replied, pleased that he understood.

He stomped out. I called after him, "Since the weather's ruined the crime scene anyway, can you lift the tape? If the power goes out, we'll need more wood, and the stacks are behind the tape."

He slammed the back door behind him. Merry, seated by the kitchen-dining windows, remarked that he was ripping off the crime scene tape.

I returned to my cleaning duties and had the blood mopped up by the time the Cortezes returned to track in mud and cold rain. The sky had started to weep fat, freezing tears. I gathered my construction project and retired to my office to let the newcomers sit together. Besides, I wanted to hear myself think.

They kept me supplied with food and drink, but I blinked when the person bearing breakfast tacos was Pastor Nathan instead of a lovely Cortez woman.

With the deprecating smile taught in seminary, he shut the door to my office and sat in the client chair directly across from me. He looked even more tired than he had yesterday.

"I didn't get a chance to talk to you or the elder Mr. Thompson before my police interview yesterday, but I took your advice and said I couldn't say anything without counsel present. I know I don't have a connection with your firm or family, but I did want to consult an attorney before speaking with them."

Now I remembered that he'd been the first one behind Officer Al yesterday when the policeman charged down the stairs to yell at me. "I've no objection to being your first attorney, as long as your interests don't conflict with my other clients. I've got a contract somewhere around here —oops, it's got icing on it. Everything's got icing on it. Sign it and hand me a retainer, and we're good."

He read the contract carefully, like it was a new translation of scripture. After he scribbled at the bottom, he handed me a crumpled five dollar bill and picked up an icing knife. "I'm happy to put in some sweat equity too, as the Habitat for Humanity people say."

"Fellow volunteer?"

"Yes, indeed. I've worked on two houses since I returned to Beauchamp. Electrician's assistant."

"Painter of high things, me. Sounds like you've got a history with this town?"

"I grew up here, left for college and other adventures, and returned last year to lead the First Baptist Church." He studied the original photo before selecting matching jellybeans for the roof. "It looks like the jellybean roof shingles were cut in two first?"

"Yes. Looks like you're an experienced candy builder."

"Vacation Bible School and Advent workshops will do that for you. You should see my pasta portraits of Jesus. Very lifelike, I'm told."

"Tell Darryl, our holiday coordinator. He'd be glad to display them on a Jesus-appropriate holiday."

"I answered questions about your Easter-Passover-Ostara display for weeks."

I winced. That ended up on the news.

"I told everyone that it seemed to be a sincere, respectful effort at honoring multiple religions, and that's what we should focus on."

"Thanks." I joined the jellybean-slicing effort. "Was there something in particular you wanted to ask me?" I could tell this was going to be one of those onion-peeling consultations.

"Because I've got a history with the town, I wasn't sure how much of it I should mention to the police."

"That depends. They're interested in everyone's relationship with the victim. Victims. But usually a recent connection is more relevant than, say, their stealing your lunch money in grammar school."

The pastor focused on sculpting a decorative cornice from the stiffening icing. You have to work fast with the stuff. "What about stealing my girlfriend in high school?"

"My general advice has been that unless it obviously relates to the present, don't volunteer ancient history to them. However, as your attorney, I want to know everything, the better to advise you what might be relevant to the investigation or a conflict of interest for me."

"It has been some time," he observed as he made a rigid line of silver candy doodads around a window. "Seventeen years." He leaned back in the chair to look me directly the eye. "Time enough for me to have become Harmony Brandon's father."

Good thing my hair's already curly, with all the hair-curling things people tell me. "Are you?"

"I don't know." He picked up a licorice stick but set it down again. "Claire and I dated in senior year—Homecoming, Prom, all the senior celebrations. After school was out, she changed. I don't know what the problem was. She said she was busy packing for the summer chef's school she was attending in a few weeks. She was like a different person every time I saw her, but I couldn't get close to any of them. We were True Love Waits kids, but one night she changed her mind. The next week she said she was dating Guy Randall and not to call her anymore. Then she went to Colorado and never came back."

"What did you do?" I asked, sorting through the candies for green Sprees and Skittles to replace shrubbery around the house. Leal Automotive had gone to a lot of trouble with their gingerbread house, which looked nothing like their grubby garage, more like a small-scale castle on the Rhine.

"Went crazy. Did drugs. I figured if this was my reward for being such a good boy all my life—I couldn't take it. It took me years to get through even junior college, and then I did auto mechanic work for a decade." His patient, pastoral mask slipped as he returned to yesteryear. He twirled licorice in his fingers. "Doug Severn was my dealer."

CHAPTER 12

"Was that unique in Beauchamp?" I asked, glad I'd had ten years' practice of listening to confidences from my friends.

"No. If you did drugs in Beauchamp, you got them from Doug."

"But Doug's not dead, so you don't need to provide any connection to him. And you obviously found your way out of drugging."

"Yes. I host an AA meeting at the church." His eyes gleamed with the fervor of one ready to tell his story.

Hoping to cut off his spiritual awakening, I pushed on. "Is there any reason to think you've been pining for Claire for seventeen years?"

"Besides my wife?"

"That would be convincing," I agreed, "though not conclusive."

"We're separated now, getting the church used to the idea. We've known for some time that our marriage was over, but she kindly stayed with me until I could get established in my new position. Now we're waiting until she decides she's ready to come out to everyone, and that's a big step. But she believes it will be a great help to LGBTQ+ people, to see how we cope with it. I confess I'm nervous about whether the church will allow me to continue as pastor after knowing our story."

"They should, unless they feel you should have converted her. She sounds like a terrific person."

"She is! I couldn't have made it through seminary without her. She was so supportive of all my dreams. How could I be any less for her? This discovery has been so painful for a girl raised in a deeply Evangelical home, yet I've never seen her happier—which makes me sad, because I was happy with her." He wasn't looking at me, but his hands were steady as he carved another cornice.

"I'm convinced you've had a full life since high school. For the moment, you can count it as distant past, subject to your eventual attorney's opinions."

"Thank you." He stood. "I hate to abandon my building project, but I should go sit with the Brandon family in their sorrow."

Realizing that "Better you than me" was not an appropriate response, I thanked him for his help and declared the mini-castle ready to go to the final decorators.

Still struggling to recapture his Christian calm, Pastor Nathan left by the front door. I frowned, wondering if he was for real or just very, very practiced. Remembering every church scandal I'd heard about, I could believe that someone could smile and spout Biblical words while doing dreadful deeds, say, like murder. What had returning to his hometown and seeing his old girlfriend, dealer, and his possible child done to him?

After seeing him out, I returned my current house back to the Candyland Sweatshop and announced that it was ready for more bedazzlement; I was moving on to the next demolished house that needed my special skills. There were at least four.

I classified the repairs as (1) decorative (missing a few candies), (2) minor structural (needing a new turret, corner, wall), (3) major structural (missing multiple elements), and (4) crumbs. I picked out a few of the third category that I could quickly make someone else's problem before returning to the hopeless cases of the fourth.

Before escaping back to my office, I announced, "We might see the police again today in the ongoing murder investigations. In expectation of that, I'd like you to record where you went to post your flyers last night."

Over the hoots and groans, Cherry demanded, "How am I supposed to do that when I'm a stranger in this town? All I know is we wandered around lost forever. I don't know what the streets were called."

Dianne was taking inventory of the construction materials. "I'll have Darryl print out maps of Beauchamp for you to draw your route. You probably have an idea which way you went for how many blocks."

"And mark who you were with," I added. "I'll print the maps. Darryl and Johnny are still in the emergency room."

I could see Dianne shaking her head and mouthing some Spanish words she wouldn't want the older generation to hear, but I couldn't hear them over the chorus of concern. She raised her voice in her second native language to say, "When I go out for more candy, I can check your routes. Most of the flyers will still be up."

"It's like you don't trust us!" wailed Juke in that extra special youngest child-in-the-family whine.

Dianne sighed down to her toes before declaring in her patented Hermana Mayor voice, two decibels quieter than a shout, "JD, please explain the concept of evidence to them. I've got to finish the candy inventory. This will be my last trip out for anything. The rain's getting worse, and it's freezing now."

Plinks and splats on Gregg House's white metal roof several stories up heralded seriously bad weather, which might last all of fifteen minutes, Texas being what it is. I shrugged amidst the excited chatter. They were all still young enough to dream of a white Christmas, the Texas unicorn.

I asked, "Ever hear of alibis? I'm trying to establish them for you. Lem Quiston went out walking yesterday evening and met his murderer. Coincidentally, around twenty of you went walking in the vicinity."

"You told us to," complained Tima.

"True, but you can't blame the police for being interested in twenty possible witnesses or potential perpetrators. If you saw anything that might bear on the case, let me know right away. Grandfather and I can't protect you if we don't know what you know. Also, on your next break after you finish your map and testimony—everyone who can should go get some wood from the piles in the backyard. I'll tape off areas inside where to put the logs. We might need extra wood if the winter storm hits us hard. That's not likely, but between our Scouting and Red Cross training, we're always prepared."

That request drew even more complaints and predictions that they'd all be stuck in this dump for a week. I scooted back to my office to print maps of Beauchamp.

After I handed them out, Dianne herded me back towards my office to ask in a low voice, "Are they in trouble? More than they were yesterday?"

"After I see their alibis, I'll let you know."

"It's not like my sisters or cousins would murder anyone," she said in a stout voice designed to convince herself more than me.

"Mine either," I agreed, while shrinking from the memory of Wild Cherry, terror of fifth grade, who blossomed after our mother died. Had she been waiting for an excuse to appear again?

Johnny wasn't there to confirm that his sister wouldn't either. I'm not sure he would have. Remembering her knife and Lem's torn sweatshirt kept me from opening my mouth. Silence lay leaden until I remembered my last conversation with Officer Al.

I took Dianne's notebook and pen and wrote *20 30.02*. "Does this mean anything to you?"

She stared hard, willing the numbers to reveal their meaning. I always caved when she stared at me like that. "Wait—I know this. Does the space between *20* and the other numbers mean anything?"

I shrugged. "No one knows anything about anything. We're all guessing."

"I know! The *30.02* is the NACE number for manufacture of computers and other information processing equipment."

"Oh?"

"You know, the European industry codes, their version of NAICS."

"Color me impressed. Does it ever occur to you that we're educated beyond usefulness?"

She looked deflated. Dianne doesn't like not knowing things.

I consoled her with, "I thought it was the burglary section of the Texas Penal Code, 30.02. I don't have any idea about the *20* either. Officer Al found a piece of paper in Lem's pocket with these numbers, but Lem wasn't studying for the bar or the CPA exam."

"Lottery number. Maybe Mississippi does theirs differently." Dianne still looked glum. "This case has nothing to do with burglary or European industry."

I was saved a response by the approach of Dianne's mother. Her house shoes tapped the wooden floor just like her party shoes.

"Lupita, how could you suspect your sisters and cousins of such a crime? They are all very hurt."

Dianne couldn't stop a soft stamp of her foot, a holdover from teenage years. "Just wait until the police get through with them! Mamí, I know your children and nieces are the most marvelous human beings ever who would never do anything wrong, but the police do not know that. If we present them with a list of our evening's activities and witnesses to them, that should be sufficient to remove them from the list of suspects. But I don't need to remind you that prisons are full of people, especially brown and Black people, who did not commit the crimes they were accused of."

"You will save them?" Mrs. Cortez turned to me with black, terrible eyes.

"I'll—I will do my best," I stammered. "I'm hoping to have them off the suspect list before it's developed, but if that doesn't happen, I'd suggest hiring an experienced defense attorney."

Bleak silence fell again until Mrs. Cortez turned to matters she could do something about. "If you're going to the dollar store, Lupita, I suggest buying heavy winter clothing, like sweatshirts and pants. None of us brought clothing for severe weather."

"That's a good idea, Mamí. That will give everyone something to sleep in, at least. I can get some stadium blankets too. I'm not sure the house can maintain comfortable warmth through the night." She took the list of sizes from her mother. "I might be a while. I'm going to follow the paths everyone said they took, to see if the fliers are still up."

"I will come with you. I can take photos of the fliers and street signs so you don't have to get out of the car." Mrs. Cortez looked relieved to have something to do besides play with peppermints.

"Thank you, Mamí." As they embraced, Dianne tried to lay her head on her mother's shoulder, which just can't be done when the daughter is half a foot taller than the mother, but Dianne never stops trying.

I watched them divvy up boots, heavy coats, hats, gloves, and scarves in preparation to leave, Mrs. Cortez making sure Dianne had the thickest boots and fabric, not to mention an extra scarf. The whole exchange reflected the entangled criticism and love in their relationship, which is why Dianne will always go home for the holidays, despite making sure to live at least three hours away.

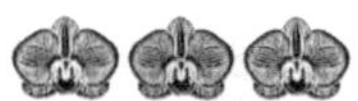

Darryl and Johnny returned shortly after Dianne and her mother departed, before the commands from those left behind died down.

"Get extra cinnamon dots! And those tiny marshmallows."

"Don't get me anything yellow. I hate yellow."

"Get extra socks. That way we can wear two pair."

"Get gloves and hats that we can wear to bed."

"See if they have blankets."

With the return of the heroes, Mrs. Ly went into full-on grandmother fuss mode, with commands to others to make hot chocolate and tea and some lunch, for heaven's sake. They must be starved. And Darryl should stand over the tile, not the wooden floor, to take off that ridiculous gear, dripping everywhere.

Because his coat wouldn't fit over all his bandages, even with his clothes cut off in strategic places, his top layer of clothing was lawn-and-leaf size garbage bags. As he divested himself of these with the help of the cousins and advice from Mrs. Ly, Johnny, still bundled, nodded to me to follow him to the clinic.

"How's Darryl?" I asked.

"He'll be fine in a few weeks with the antibiotics and tetanus shot. I don't want to ask him to help me. Would you? Godzilla is still free in the clinic, though I hope he's calmed down."

"We're not going to bathe him, are we?"

Johnny considered. "We might have to wipe the blood off. And the icing from yesterday. We shouldn't oil him unless we give him a full bath. You'll want to put on your coat, maybe leather work gloves."

"So I can get my one winter coat shredded?"

"So you can keep your skin from being shredded or punctured. I think there's a reason we haven't heard from Godzilla's owner." After I bundled up and bid a silent farewell to my coat, he opened the clinic door and whispered, "Move quietly and slowly. We don't want to startle him."

"That we do not," I agreed with fervor, wincing at the pounding rain and sleet on the roof. A different sound than hurricanes make, but still threatening.

The din was louder in here because the clinic's metal porch roof was closer to us than the roof of the main house. The racket made it hard to identify the constant low rumble. Some kind of machinery two steps from malfunction?

We took a few more steps in, past his office, to the main entry area. Now we could hear soft soprano singing, familiar to those of us who've been in a band with her for a decade.

Chantal was sitting on the floor, her back against the front door, singing a lullaby to the pink bundle in her arms, a bright contrast to her nut-brown skin. Godzilla glared in our general direction. I pulled out my phone in slo-mo and snapped a photo of this alternative Virgin Mary and Demon Child.

"And I'm gonna make you some little jimjams to keep you warm in this nasty weather. Have another treat. You gotta keep up your strength and pile on a few pounds for the winter." She reached into the cat treat jar, open on the floor beside her.

He snatched the cat treat from her hand and nuzzled her chin. The malfunctioning machine, now louder, was his purr.

"Don't y'all scare him now," she sang to us in the same sweet voice, but with threatening undertones.

Johnny glided forward one step but stopped as the purr shifted to a growl and Godzilla's skin rippled like pink waves along his back. "I haven't finished his intake exam. Could I coach you through it? From across the room? He's had enough trauma since he arrived. Before too."

"Not sticking a thermometer up his butt. None of us want that, right, pretty boy?"

I tried to see Godzilla as she did and failed.

On the opposite side of the room, Johnny pulled out instruments of his trade and put them on a tray. "No, you can just stick this in his ear." He held up something that looked like a toy gun and then a stethoscope. "And I'll want you to listen to his heart and lungs, if he'll stop purring and/or growling." He pushed the tray across the examination island toward Chantal.

Godzilla laid his ears flat. Johnny stepped back.

I edged toward the door. "Looks like you have this situation under control. Call if you need me. By the way, Johnny, Officer Al came by. He wants our photos."

Johnny waved a hand, which could have been dismissive or affirming, but definitely indicated a lack of interest as he scrutinized Chantal and Godzilla.

"I'm just gonna set you on this table here with your warm blankie, and we'll take the treats with us. The good boy can have all the treats, all the treats, yes he can."

I did not want to see this.

CHAPTER 13

Back in the living room-gallery, a bright fire crackled in the fireplace. A couple of Cortez cousins, huddled at the back windows, exclaimed over the snow and wondered whether it would stick long enough to cover the winter-brown grass. What hopeful children.

Near the fireplace someone had placed the only modern piece of furniture in the house, a super recliner bought when Johnny broke his leg in a losing argument with a wild hog. Darryl's crinkly locks peeked out from under a stack of blankets, and I could hear his wheedling tones.

"Miss Claire, I hurt so bad. Do you think I could have one of your special chocolates?"

The woman who handed him a cup of hot cocoa—I hoped it was only cocoa—was indeed Claire Brandon, newly arrived since my brief tenure as vet tech. I looked up and down the gallery and saw that she'd brought Harmony and the four Quiston children, who sat at the main kitchen table as the grannies fussed over them. The children looked shocked, their grief ranging from Harmony's minimal to Mary's full-on gush of tears. The boys, whom I hadn't learned to individually identify, did their best to uphold the honor of stoic Southern manhood, but at least two had red-rimmed eyes.

I felt a deep stab of empathy and sympathy down to my core, because my own mother died when I was nineteen, but that didn't give me the magic words to say to these young people, just the knowledge that there are no magic words.

I don't know how long I watched them not eat the food placed beside them, not repair the gingerbread houses in front of them, not respond to anything said to them, but when I looked away, Darryl was lying back in the recliner with a beatific expression on his face as he savored chocolates from the tray Claire Brandon set beside him.

"Thank you sooooooooooo much, Ms. Brandon," he mumbled with a full mouth and eyes closed.

I tell my friends not to commit crimes where I can see them, since I'm an officer of the court (by some definitions) and need plausible deniability. Serving a nineteen-year-old cannabis edibles in a state where marijuana is illegal except for restricted cases of medical diagnosis left me no deniability at all. I sighed and stepped forward to intercept Claire before she could return to the kitchen.

"May I speak with you in my office, Claire?" I placed myself so she'd have to knock me down or run a wide end-around to do otherwise.

"I'd be happy to, JD. There's something I need to talk to you about." She glanced over her shoulder at her younger family. "Thank you for welcoming the children. I thought it would be best for them to leave the house for a while. My sister—isn't doing well, and they don't need that memory on top of everything else. I doubt they'll contribute much to your reconstruction effort, though."

"I'm glad if there's anything we can do to help. Everyone says they want to at such a time, but what do they even mean? After the hundredth time or so someone said that to me after my mother died, I wanted to scream, 'What do you think you can do? Dig her grave? Mother her children?'"

"Casseroles. And pound cake. The Southern answer to everything." Her voice lacked its normal lilt, and her smile looked like an understudy's version of the real Claire. But her family had suffered a shocking loss, no matter how any of them felt about Lem Quiston, and I hadn't noticed much connection or affection between Claire and Lem. I didn't see how there could be, with them living in separate states and this being the first year Lem came to Texas for Christmas.

"I'm sure we'll provide one or the other or both. Johnny keeps a few pound cakes in the freezer for such occasions. He's figured out that most people here aren't vegetarians and therefore aren't in the market for his eggplant lasagna or six-bean casseroles." As we took our seats on either side of my desk, I realized my error. Having a gingerbread house project between you makes gravitas harder. "Claire, I know he's in pain and shock, but Darryl's only nineteen, not old enough for cannabis even if it were legal in Texas."

Her laugh was a brief return to the spontaneity of Real Claire, though it might not have lasted as long as normal. I was glad; I suspected I was going to feel like an idiot soon.

"Thank you, JD. I needed that, though of course Mother and Melanie would be horrified. Melanie would never forgive me, but she never has anyway. Maybe someday I'll know what for." She wiped her eyes. "People forget that I *can* bake without cannabis, and after Mother told me about the mixup last year, I thought I'd better bring some perfectly straight products."

"He looked blissed out."

"Probably due to a certain power of suggestion, certainly not from any chemical in five minutes."

Boy, was my face red. Or it should have been. "My apologies for leaping to conclusions."

"Accepted. You were more polite about it than many people, including —are you tired of hearing this?—my sister, who will hardly let her kids accept food from my hands, so sure she is that I've laced it with gateway drugs."

"That must make mealtimes awkward."

"Not really. It just gets me out of kitchen duty when she's around." Her smile faded as she turned her head to gaze out the windows that surround the circular wall of my office.

Unlike the younger generation out in the gallery, she didn't exclaim at the snow's progress. In other seasons, a glance out those windows provides a riot of color, but now the trees were stripped to bare sticks, except for one yaupon holly on the south corner, its red berries clinging to naked branches, a lonely attempt at holiday cheer.

She turned her gaze forward again, eyeing the gingerbread repairs instead of meeting my eyes. She studied the photo and the house's current condition, now moved from crumb status to "has walls." She picked up a pastry knife. "May I?"

I replied, noticing that she didn't wait for an answer before dipping it in the icing, "Of course. My skills are structural, not decorative." As she focused on sculpting chimney decorations with the same intensity that I'd given the bar exam, I gave her a verbal nudge. "You have something else to say to me?"

She swiped a cornice into being. This house was going to look better than the original. "I do. I don't know how much you know about me."

"Younger daughter of David and Leigh Brandon, went to Colorado after high school in Beauchamp, went to baking college there, married, had Harmony, buried your husband at a young age, opened a cannabis bakery in 2012 when recreational marijuana became legal." Because of client confidentiality, I didn't mention anything Pastor Nathan said.

"That's all true. Now let me fill in the gaps." She jammed little silver balls into the icing. "Nathan and I dated senior year, though we promised not to get serious because we knew we'd be at different colleges later. I was going to what my family called 'Cake Camp' in June after graduation, because I wanted a taste of—" A trace of her old grin flickered for a nanosecond. "—the baking life. My parents didn't consider cooking school as real college, but I'd gotten them to agree to this much at least." She stopped talking to focus on carving the icing door, worthy of any Gothic cathedral. "In the riotous month of pleasure before Cake Camp started, Mother asked me to go with Melanie to a party. Mother had no problem forbidding us to do things, but she usually tried a softer approach first. 'Take your sister' was one of her misguided favorites, in the belief that Melanie and I would look out for each other. The way it worked was that we'd ignore each other from the moment we walked in the door. So, as much as I'd like to blame Melanie, I'm sure she was off with Lem, in ignorance of what was happening to me, at least until afterwards. I've never known if she shared the secrets of the Three Amigos."

The more she talked, the more her face drained of any good cheer, making her unrecognizable. "I was an Awana—a Baptist achievement award for girls, involving scripture memorization and charitable works that culminates in a grand ball, formal dresses and all. I received the grand prize for the most scripture verses ever memorized and my crowning achievement of baking birthday cakes for everyone in the Shady Rest Seniors Home for a year. But the words *date rape* never appeared in any of those scriptures, certainly not *date rape drug*. It would be years before I learned them. At the time I called myself an unfaithful girlfriend, a slut, and worse, for having sex for the first time with Guy Randall. Nathan wasn't there that night—he was at work—but I tried to make it up to him the next time I saw him. I couldn't tell anybody. Certainly not Mother, who dragged the whole family to church Sunday morning, Sunday evening, and Wednesday evening. Not my father, who took me to the Purity Ball when I was ten and put a ring on my finger and told me I was his until he transferred me to my husband."

Her eyes met mine briefly before she examined the few tools I had for sculpting icing. She looked like she was picking out a makeup brush.

"Harmony did not attend a Purity Ball." White blobs over gingerbread windows turned into Baroque swirls. "A few weeks into Cake Camp —the highlight of my life so far—I knew I was never going home, not pregnant. My parents would want me to carry the baby to term and give it to strangers. With my background, I couldn't contemplate abortion either, though I did lie in my dorm room at night and scheme how to get the money." She sighed, pushing her creation toward me. She leaned back into the comfort of the velvet chair. I'd never seen her look that sad.

"Short version: I took a few weeks' training as a home health aide for hospice and was assigned to Don Schuyler, a man in his forties, dying of cancer. He asked me one day what I was going to do about the baby   it wasn't hard to figure out I was pregnant, when I spent more time vomiting than he did. He had no family but had a comfortable amount of money and wanted to do something worthwhile with it, like change a young girl's life for the better. He'd pay for an abortion if I wanted. If I wanted to have the baby, he'd make me his beneficiary and heir, even marry me if I didn't mind, to streamline the money process. I didn't want to marry someone for his money, but he pointed out that if that money were my goal, he was a poor catch. He tried not to show it, but I could see how excited he was about having a family, and I said yes. This baby deserved somebody to be excited about her. I told my parents I'd fallen in love, but he had cancer, so we were getting married and having a baby right away. And I couldn't come home because he couldn't travel. And they couldn't come see me just now because he was very fragile from his treatment. I never knew I had that many lies in me. Later they did come, when Don was 'better.'"

"Through Cake Camp, I connected with medical marijuana dispensaries, where I learned to make edibles for patients like Don. He consumed most of my output at first, but later it was an important source of income for me." She looked out the window again, and I knew she was staring into the past rather than at the yaupon holly berries. "He used to apologize for living longer than the six months his doctor expected. Many terminal patients do live longer once they have the good care hospice provides, and he finally had the family he wanted. He adored Harmony and treasured every day with her. We had three Christmases together. I only wish we'd had more. I wish she had the chance to remember him."

She turned back and placed all her implements and supplies in a row. She looked up to meet my eyes with a burning intensity. "As far as my parents are concerned and all of Beauchamp, I thought, Don Schuyler is Harmony Schuyler Brandon's father. Imagine my surprise at the open house yesterday when I heard Lem say to his friends, with that skin-crawling laugh of his, 'She looks just like her father.'"

I remembered Sophie Thi's opinion of Lem's laughter.

"They were looking at Harmony, hanging out with her cousin Mary near the front door. Did they know I was nearby? I don't know; their backs were to me."

I cleared my throat. "Actually, she doesn't—whoever her father is. She looks like you and Miss Leigh, except for the freckles across her nose. More to the point, who besides Lem, Guy, and Doug would suspect her parentage?"

"Melanie? But I can't believe she wouldn't have taunted me over the years. She was thrilled when I told Mother and Daddy I was getting married. They wouldn't let her marry Lem until she finished college, but she threw such a fit when I got married right out of high school that they let her and Lem get married before she finished her last semester. She was even happier that I couldn't come back for the wedding and Mother couldn't make me her maid of honor. But she would have never let me hear the end of it for 'having' to get married. Unless these guys told other friends—and I think I would have heard about it over the years—only the three of them. And two of them are dead."

That reminded me of a certain saying about secrets.

Claire continued, "Yesterday I didn't see any point in bringing up ancient history, but now I wonder if the police might see a possible motive for my killing two of the three people who know a secret I'd rather reveal in my own time."

"They might, but I don't see any reason to provide it to them. I'd rather they find evidence first."

"Neither my daughter nor my mother know. I was thinking about telling them this year, if Melanie went home before Christmas early, like usual. The past was already intruding on me, you see. Mother's been telling me all year that Nathan's come back to town as the senior minister of our church, what a great job he's doing, and won't I be glad to see him." She took a deep breath. "No, actually. I've tried to avoid him. It's possible that he's Harmony's father. Or someone from Cake Camp. I just didn't care anymore, you know? What was even the point?"

The longer she talked, the more her face twisted in pain.

"Did you not want to do a DNA test?"

"I didn't want her in a database, not unless I could be sure that she wouldn't be revealed to a bunch of new relatives. When it came down to it, I just didn't care enough to try. She's my daughter, and that's all that matters to me."

The back door opened, heralding the voyagers' return. Even louder were the exclamations as fourteen young women fell upon bags of clothes with glee, even for dollar store sweats. It beat laboring in the Candyland Sweatshop. I tapped a quick text to Dianne.

To give Claire's thoughts a different direction, I said, "Yesterday you told us when and where you observed Guy. Would you mind sitting down with Dianne to sketch out your actions? We'll look for witnesses to confirm, to protect you if that becomes necessary. We'll do this with everyone in case there's other possible suspects—and to keep the focus off of you."

I heard Dianne's footsteps approaching, and I went to waylay her. Shutting the heavy office door behind me, I gave her a quick rundown of what I wanted, and she turned pale.

"JD, do you know how many people are staying in this house? And might you possibly be able to contribute to the effort?"

"Of course I can. Darryl too. Maybe my grandfather."

"Darryl closed his eyes when I walked by and hid his phone under the blanket. And why not Johnny?"

"He's a suspect. I don't think Darryl is, but we should give him time off after his workplace injury."

"That cat!"

"Forget the cat. The cat has an alibi. Let's focus on possible suspects who don't: Claire, Sophie Thi, Cherry, Tima, Juke, Johnny, and his grandmother."

"Johnny's grandmother has a motive?"

"Yes. She always sees everything anyway, which is good, because we need to pick up info about those not here: Nathan, Miss Leigh, Melanie, and Doug. Can you think of anyone else?"

"The rest of Beauchamp, since they were all here yesterday. They're more likely than my sisters."

"My sister too, I'm almost positive." I winced and crossed my fingers. "As long as we can establish that the murderer isn't one of ours, I don't care if the mayor and the town council did it, all holding the knife together. You start with Claire, and I'll start with Tima or Juke. We shouldn't question our own sisters."

"You've already got Claire. Why didn't you get started already? Do you realize how long this is going to take?"

I grimaced. "Before we apply for Medicare, I hope. I didn't start with Claire because I absolutely believe everything she says and want to defend her with my life. That's why I'll have Grandfather go with her if the police want to talk to her again."

Dianne supplied a couple of curses in Spanish. "That's all we need. Minimum, she's ten years older than you."

"Is that a problem? It *is* the twenty-first century."

"Let's start with she's your client and a suspect in a murder case. I didn't know the suspect part, but you said so. If she is, why is she here and not at the police station?"

"Because Officer Al hasn't figured it out yet. With any luck, he won't, but I want to be ready." My phone sang its tune, and I answered it. Dianne gave me a poisonous look, with the weather providing a punctuating clap of thunder, as she went to her office to retrieve her laptop.

Officer Al barked (with his dog Cupcake yipping in the background), "JD, what have you done with Claire Brandon? I need to talk to her right away. If you're hiding a suspect, I'll have you disbarred."

CHAPTER 14

I shook my head in resignation and took a few steps away. It never works to rely on police stupidity.

I infused my voice with surprise. "Suspect? She's a suspect? I hadn't heard. As for where she is, you know they just had a death in the family. I'd be surprised if you could talk to any of them." You might have noticed I did not make any claims about where she was or wasn't.

"I've learned that the death is mighty convenient for her."

"Her brother-in-law?"

"Both deaths, actually. I want to talk to her."

"Well, sure you would. Let me talk to my grandfather. He's going to handle her case."

Officer Al gulped and forgot his badass training. "Good God, JD! Don't do that. That old man scares me."

"That was his job as a U.S. Attorney."

"By the time I got through yesterday's interviews with him there, I was ready to arrest myself. Come on, it's just a few questions. You can handle those."

"Sounds like the client would be better served by my grandfather. I'm working on the voice and the glare, but I know I'm not there yet."

"JD, it's just something I have to follow up on, just to say I did."

"You know, if you'd tell me what's going on, then we could decide what level of representation she needs."

He was silent. I thought I could hear him trembling under the storm growling outdoors and pounding on the roof.

"Look, JD, I think it's ridiculous."

"No doubt."

"But I have to follow leads even when I know they're stupid."

Especially when you don't have anything else, I thought, with an anxious look out the window. As a Houston native, I've spent many a miserable day watching for hurricanes. My rational brain told me it was too late in the year for those storms; my child self said SHUTUP-SHUTUPSHUTUP. The whole Gulf Coast has permanent PTSD from bad storms.

"Someone asked for police protection this morning because with two of his friends dead, he was afraid Claire Brandon would come after him."

"Just spitballing here—someone who might be a six-foot-tall buff guy, maybe associated with real estate and construction. Let's call him Doug. And he needs police protection from a five-foot-six dainty lady who bakes cookies for a living."

"When you put it like that—"

"I do put it like that."

"But a cook would have access to knives."

"Which she carries with her to Christmas parties far away from her own bakery? Or are we going to include everyone who fixes their own dinner? I'm trying to go along here, but I can't imagine why Claire Brandon would come home for Christmas and start murdering people, including her own brother-in-law."

"They knew a terrible secret about her, and she was afraid they'd tell."

"Oh? Some secret they just found out? How would they do that, when she lives in Colorado? Or something they knew from her childhood in Beauchamp, decades ago? Why would they tell it now? There's a word, right on the tip of my tongue—What is it when someone threatens to make public something you'd rather they didn't? Aren't there laws against such things?"

"JD, don't be—"

"Blackmail! That's it. Maybe you should investigate that. Ms. Brandon might want to look into filing for slander or libel too. I look forward to discovery."

"I didn't say anything like that. I just need to check her alibi. Alibis. Like I would for anybody near the case."

"Just doing her first. I see. I can give her a partial alibi for the party. She attended with her whole family, arriving near opening time and staying until the end. Because she brought treats from her bakery, she interacted with our party staff, helping out where she could. Lem left first, and the rest didn't leave until you interviewed them. I imagine she has an alibi for the evening from her family. But you're investigating whether she killed Guy Randall at the party and went home to kill her brother-in-law with a pastry knife in the evening or next morning—I'm not sure when he died—not even in the home where they were staying, but three blocks away? I'm sure you'll find someone who remembers them taking a walk together, when they'd barely spoken twenty words in twenty years. By the way, I've been working with pastry knives this afternoon. They cut soft butter and icing, nothing else."

The lights flickered. I could hear the intake of breath from the icing workers down the hall; it was late enough in the day that the room dimmed. I appreciated Nature accompanying my stirring statements.

"It's more complicated than that."

"It has to be, because I cannot imagine what on the Central Texas scorched earth could anyone think they have to say about Claire Brandon that she would care about? She owns a cannabis bakery in Colorado, where that's legal. Half of Beauchamp thinks that classifies her with the Whore of Babylon. The other half wishes she'd be their dealer, which she will not do, being a law-abiding citizen. Point is, there's nothing that could be said about her that hasn't been said. If gossip bothered her, she'd never come home. She visits her mother only once or twice a year anyway, usually without her brother-in-law."

The lights went out for several seconds, theatrically appropriate for the officer's silence. The candy crew exclaimed, loud enough for Darryl to blink and stir in his chair.

After a long sigh, Officer Al whispered, as though Cupcake cared, "JD, you can't tell anybody this, but it's about her daughter."

"I wouldn't tell anybody, and I'd file suit against anybody who said anything publicly. Not against you, of course. You're just doing your duty and keeping confidences where you can. But if you've got anything to say about a sixteen-year-old girl, you'd better keep it low. Not only because we're talking about a child, but because nothing those guys think they know could possibly be true."

The lights went out again, with a finality. A chorus at the other end of the house shrieked as the house plunged into darkness. I counted to ten, and when I had no lights other than twenty cell phones, I said into my phone, "We're dealing with a blackout here. I've got to go. Your person-of-interest isn't going anywhere. She's dealing with a blackout too, plus death of a near family member, plus Christmas with her family. Merry Christmas to you too, in case I don't talk to you before then, though you're welcome to come to the concert on Monday. Mrs. Ly's taking attendance, you know."

I ended the call and jumped when I saw Dianne and Claire right behind me in the doorway. They'd been there long enough for Claire's eyes to fill with pain and gratitude.

"Thank you," she whispered.

"Just doing his job." Dianne dismissed my efforts. As the panic around us swelled, she added, "I better get our emergency procedures in place before this lot loses it. You'd think they'd never been in a power outage before."

Being in Texas, of course they had. But even my soul cringed at the question of how long it would last. Sure, we had supplies. We had procedures (because Dianne, you know?), but would our Christmas dinner be cans of cold beans in the dark, after we burned all our candles and Sterno? What about our elders? Could they tough it out?

Claire broke into my reverie—okay, panic. "Should I expect a visit from Officer Al?"

"At some point, if only because he has to talk with Lem's family."

"He did that this morning. That's what set Melanie foaming, which ended the interview."

"Police talk to you multiple times after a suspicious death, but I'm not sure how much he'll be investigating in a snow storm." Spying Johnny emerging from the clinic with a flashlight, I called, "Johnny, any news?"

He shied away from the noise and confusion and joined us. "I was able to get a few feet closer to him, but not within touching distance. It will be a slow process to build his trust. I hope Chantal will stay until that happens."

I spoke to Claire's utter bewilderment in a measured, controlled voice. "The cat that crashed our party, going by the name of Godzilla. He's not the friendliest, as attested by Darryl's wounds. We're trying to find his owner."

Johnny frowned. "I'm not sure we want to. Where did Godzilla learn this conduct if not at his home?"

I closed my eyes against the thought of the feline hell on wheels taking up residence. The Very Good Kitties would have something to say about that. "Johnny, I know you're concerned about Godzilla, and you should be. But have you heard anything from the medical examiner about Lem? Do they have a cause of death? I'm hoping for a heart attack instead of murder."

"Communications are sparse on Sunday, but the ME will keep me informed. Do you know about Empress Elisabeth?"

"Queen of the UK?" I asked. "Did she get a promotion? Bout time; she's been queen since before my grandmother was born. Wait, is she even alive?"

"No, Empress of Austria, died in the nineteenth century. Never mind. We should help Dianne." He drifted away.

Claire stared after him with narrowed eyes. "I should take the children home."

I wasn't sure if she meant because of the blackout or because this place was nuts. "Do you need anything?"

She shook her head. "Daddy believed in Y2K and had a generator put in both at the farm and the house in town. And of course Mother's bought out all the surrounding grocery stores before Christmas. We'll be fine."

CHAPTER 15

Claire pasted on her trademarked smile and called to the third-generation Brandons. Our sisters and cousins made a big deal of thanking them for their help while distributing their outerwear. Tears ran down Mary Quiston's cheeks while her Aunt Claire told them about the generator their granddaddy put in and promised pizza and popcorn for the evening. As a long-time Colorado resident, Claire was probably the only person in town not intimidated by the winter roads.

My own sister—Cherry, of course—sneered under Dianne's directions, though her voice squinched higher than usual. "You guys have emergency plans? The only one we ever had as kids was 'Run to the neighbor's house.'"

Remembering all the howling storms when I sat with my younger sisters under a blanket fort, I put an arm around her to soften my retort. "With two Boy Scouts, including one Eagle, and Dianne the Uber-Organizer (and former Camp Fire kid), not to mention graduates of Red Cross disaster training because this house is a community shelter, yeah, we've got emergency plans. I hope you like Vienna sausages. I just don't know if they'll scale up for this many people."

With Cherry trembling against me. I looked around for Merry. She doesn't make as much noise as Cherry, but she feels deeper. From her seat at the dining table, she gave me a thumbs up with the hand that wasn't gripping Grandmother's.

Dianne raised her voice, "Power could come back on any minute, but we're going to act like it won't. We have generators for the cat shelter out back and the clinic, so those areas will be warm, but your bedrooms will be cold with no heat."

"You have generators for the cats?" asked her sister Juke, not pleased.

Beside her, Sophie Thi snorted. "In my brother's house? Of course."

Dianne continued, "There's double fireplaces on all three floors. We'll gather our beds around them and sleep in the heaviest clothes we have with as many blankets as possible. We should be able to keep the fires going with all the wood we brought in today, added to what we already had. We have chargers and independent power supplies too. The emergency supplies are in Chantal's bedroom—Where is Chantal?"

Cherry sniffed. "Playing with that beast of a cat. Every time we needed something, we had to drag her out of the clinic."

Dianne slammed her folder on the table and strode toward the clinic like an invading force. "She can play with him later. We need her now."

Johnny and Darryl called out after her, Darryl warning her to stay away from the dangerous animal, Johnny urging her not to scare Godzilla.

Dianne was back in five minutes with a disgruntled Chantal in tow.

"He didn't eat you?" Darryl was surprised.

"I hope you didn't scare him." Johnny was severe. "He's had enough trauma in his short life. He's not much more than a kitten."

Dianne gave them both a withering glare. "He's ugly as mud, but he's a perfectly nice cat. I don't know what's wrong with you guys."

"She walked right up to him and petted him," Chantal said. "He purred and let her hold him."

Dianne's wrinkled nose told me how much she enjoyed that. Johnny's brow furrowed, but he said nothing as Dianne and Chantal swung into distribution, schedules, and orders. Chantal, a New Orleans native whose family fled to Houston after Hurricane Katrina, knows that busy prep work holds back storm terrors. I gave her a quick hug in passing.

Soon I was hauling beds and rearranging furniture in Mrs. Ly's bedroom, one of the rooms with a fireplace. The older people would sleep there. When she and her husband could no longer handle stairs, they had a wall knocked out between two downstairs bedrooms and moved their lives to the first floor, an option in a 4000-square-foot home.

The power stayed off. After Chantal distributed the flashlights, the place looked like an infestation of giant fireflies. Everyone cheered up when they realized that all their essential needs would be provided: food, a place to charge their phones and devices (on a rotating schedule), and a reasonably warm place to sleep.

Amid the plans for cocoa, popcorn, and marshmallows on the third floor, Cherry announced, more cheerful now that we were actually doing things—maybe even making blanket forts. "It will be like a slumber party. Sophie Thi, you're coming with us, right? We missed you last night."

Sophie Thi traced the floor with one booted toe. "I have to stay with my grandmother."

"Go on with your friends," called Mrs. Ly from the kitchen, where she was sorting through the cans that contained our dinner. "I'll have plenty of people nearby."

Sophie Thi's face blazed with terror. Then she stomped a foot and declared, "There's no sense in him being dead if I'm still going to be afraid. Yeah, I'm coming upstairs." She charged for the stairs.

"I'll go with you." Johnny was right behind her.

Unsure yet supportive, the rest of the younger generation thundered behind. There was a pileup when she stopped to stare at Johnny.

"Why?"

"Many children's books advised me that I should take care of my little sister, and since I didn't then, I want to now."

"Stuff it, Johnny." She continued the climb to the third floor. So did Johnny.

I trailed the group with a frown. I was used to awkward expressions from the Ly siblings, but Sophie Thi's statement was an odd one to make in the middle of a murder investigation. I knew why she didn't want to go to the third floor and why she'd been sleeping on the first floor in her grandmother's room, her grandmother being still spry and able to take care of herself, as she proved every day in her senior village apartment in Austin.

Sure enough, as the crowd flowed around Sophie Thi standing just a few steps beyond the doorway, she whispered, "It was here. This was Grandpa Ky's meditation room. It was bare except for a short table with religious doodads—his altar, I guess. Doug stood by the fireplace and sniggered, saying it was his turn next. He kept running his hands over those white bricks. I wonder why I remember that. Then I grabbed the statue."

Johnny scrutinized the bricks around the fireplace while he piled kindling and logs for a fire. The third floor would hold its heat the longest, but I agreed that starting a fire before it got cold was a good idea. It's easier to keep a place warm than to make one warm.

Johnny glanced back at Sophie Thi, now surrounded by Tima, Juke, and Cherry, whispering sympathy. He pulled out his handy pocket tool, useful for any task. While he poked at a brick with the screwdriver option, I joined him by the fireplace, with the intent of blocking Sophie Thi's view. She didn't need to see her brother reenacting her abuser's actions.

Up close, I could see cracks around the brick as he pried through the mortar. It took him forever to get the brick loose enough to pull out. Everyone stopped breathing while he peered in the small hole that contained—

"Nothing." His voice was flat.

Amid the sighs of disappointment—surely there should be a portal to another world at minimum—he removed his headlamp flashlight to aim it directly in the hole and in its corners. The audience lost interest and chattered about marshmallows and cocoa while he felt around inside the hole. He pulled out his hand, covered with thin white scratches from the bricks, and aimed the light inside again. This time he used two fingers to lift something from the very back.

He held out his hand to show me—and now everyone pushed in closer. An antique ring glittered in his hand. I was betting the diamonds were real.

Johnny sighed. "I should have worn my crime scene gloves."

I suggested, "Let's show this ring to your grandmother. She might recognize it."

Johnny frowned. "She hasn't been on the third floor in years. My grandfather was the only person who ever used it regularly, as his meditation room, but not after Grandmother built the meditation building in the back for a Christmas present one year."

My brain refused to process a Jewish woman giving a Buddhist man a Christmas present, but cultures and religions often collided in the Ly family.

Johnny continued as he looked around. "We'll have to ask Grandmother how often she used it for disaster housing. My father and aunt had sleepovers up here as children, and sometimes I used it as a playroom, but I can't think of any reason anyone would have had such a ring and hid it here."

The room was a big contrast to the rest of the corniced and crenellated house, with plain, whitewashed walls and rough, wooden floors, unlike the polished floors downstairs. In the house's earliest days, it provided servants' quarters, being lined with bedrooms around the perimeter where the roof sloped. The elder Mr. Ly claimed the central room as his meditation room, and the bedrooms morphed into storage rooms for discards of their family life. The central room had also served as a community dorm during disasters, which is why it was equipped with cots and so on. Now it served as rough but adequate housing for our elves for a few days—come to think of it, returning it to its original use as servants' quarters.

We pushed our way to the door through the chatter. "Except it would be an excellent hiding place for those reasons: no one comes here, and no one could be associated with the ring. Could it have been a present from your grandfather to your grandmother, only he forgot he'd bought it by the time the occasion came around?"

"Being from wartime Vietnam, my grandfather never forgot anything he bought, especially not presents." Johnny's voice was distracted; he was looking at Sophie Thi, still and unhappy among all the movement and chatter. "I set up my building kits and science projects in this room, glad to have a quiet place where Sophie Thi would never come. I didn't understand why."

We made it to the door, but Johnny still hesitated. Looking at Sophie Thi's face, twisted with determined courage, I called out in my courtroom voice, which I have to use even with just my two sisters, "There's too many of you to keep warm by the fire. Those in the back row beds are going to be chilly. How about half of you come down to the second-floor social room?"

The second floor is laid out on a similar plan, bedrooms around a large central room (our personal living room), but the bedrooms are larger, and everything is more decorative, though less so than the first floor. Dianne's room, the master bedroom, shares the fireplace with the living room.

The idea went over well, and Johnny and I made our escape in the verbal volley as they decided who would sleep where. I carried with me the mental photo of Sophie Thi's relieved, relaxed face—the one person I knew for sure would sleep on the second floor. I couldn't be sorry about intervening, even if she was a murderer.

CHAPTER 16

On the first floor, Zap and the male cousins were still moving beds into Mrs. Ly's room. We were far enough away that I couldn't see their expressions when I told them that their assistance would be welcome with moving half of the third-floor cots down to the second, but the bed they were carrying hit the floor with a bang. I ran into a night table they'd shoved into the hall and might have heard snickering. Thereafter we trained our flashlights so we could dance around the rest of Mrs. Ly's bedroom furniture as we headed for the cluster of lights at the dining table.

The elders were bagging the repaired houses that we'd return to their homes tomorrow, assuming many things, including the weather and condition of the roads. Even two inches of snow incapacitates Texas. We don't have snowplows or salt, and people don't know how to drive in snow. They can't drive in bright, clear daylight either, but they're worse in snow. Besides, if you can't take off work or close your business for a snow day, when can you?

Dianne stood behind Mrs. Ly as they consulted the master list that matched houses with their builders. They both looked up when Johnny set the ring in front of his grandmother.

"Grandmother, have you ever—"

His words were lost when she cried out in pain. She turned the ring over and over in her hand. "Where did you get this?"

Johnny tried to explain, but she kept talking. "This was my mother's, from her mother. I inherited her jewelry when you were small. Were there any more pieces? "

"No, just—"

"There should have been several bracelets in this set, dangling earrings, and a big collar of diamonds. Then there were the sapphires, and some smaller ruby pieces. All of it was stolen, probably that dreadful summer. When I went to get it for insurance reappraisal, I couldn't find any of it. I put it away in one of my special hiding places when I received it. Summers were always so busy, trying to get things done before the school year, having you children here to visit—I didn't look for the jewelry again until that fall. We installed the safe after that. Too late."

"Would this have been the year Sophie Thi was five? I was almost eight, and I went to the restaurant with Grandfather Ky most days. She usually stayed at home or went with you on your errands."

Mrs. Ly sat back and closed her eyes. Her expression changed as she pulled up raveled threads from the past and rewove them into coherence. "John Ky, how did you know?"

"I didn't."

"That was when—I was so concerned about Sophie Thi that I let everything else go. After I put the jewelry away, it went right out of my mind until months later. It went out of my house too."

"At one point it was hidden in the bricks by the upstairs fireplace. The ring must have fallen out—it was way in the back, behind some of the concrete jags," Johnny flexed his hand with the scratches, now thin red lines. "Perhaps you could make a list of who had access to the house during that time."

Her face twisted into grimmer lines. "I already have it, and it's a short one. With two of them dead now and twenty years later, I don't know what can be done. The jewelry's never shown up anywhere."

Dianne folded her arms across her chest and stared into the darkness

—into her secret realm of numbers, I knew. In a faraway singsong, she asked, "So what happened to the rest of the jewelry?"

"How can we tell that after twenty years?" asked Mrs. Ly.

"It's reasonable to think they didn't take it to hide somewhere. There are other ways to profit that wouldn't involve presenting a whole recognizable piece or set for sale. Who magically got enough money to buy a car, start a business, splurge outside their income?"

"Got cancer treatment for a relative, went to college, adopted a child," I contributed.

Dianne looked at the ceiling. I couldn't tell whether she was disgusted or imploring a deity. "JD, you'd be amazed at how often people do not commit crimes for lofty purposes."

"Just giving people the benefit of the doubt. Can you track the proceeds of this theft?"

"I'm a forensic accountant. Of course I can. A better question would be, can I do so with the information available to me? If not, I hope I can get enough for Alejandro to get warrants." She smiled at the elders around at the table. The women being from the generation when their career options were secretary, teacher, or nurse, Dianne might as well have announced that she was a giraffe. "I keep telling my friends that forensic accounting isn't about finding a treasure map with X marks the spot of corruption. It's more like you're looking at boringly standard records, and you see something odd from the corner of your eye. So you turn and study it, and you see something else from the corner of your eye. You keep turning to look at these odd flares at the corner of your vision, and eventually they add up to a complete picture. I'm hoping to get at least an outline with publicly available information. In fact—let me look at the list of gingerbread house deliveries again."

While Dianne leaned over the list, crossing out and adding names, I remarked, "That assumes we can get out of the driveway tomorrow and that anyplace will open."

She shook her head. "JD, if you wake up on Monday morning and your bank is closed for any reason besides a bank holiday, the apocalypse is here, and you have other problems to attend to."

We acted like it was the apocalypse now and the power would be out forever. The weather played along, despite expectations that when we got all the beds in place, the lights would suddenly flare on. They didn't, so we ate cold food and drifted to the gallery fireplace to play board games, some from our college years at Casa Cortez, some from the Lys' stash going back to Johnny's father's childhood. We set up a card table closer to the fire so that the elders could play bridge, and my dear, sweet, forgetful grandmother proceeded to wipe the floor with everyone. When they switched to poker, younger people joined. Grandmother took them to the cleaners too. If only chips were money.

Then Grandmother, being the gracious Southern lady she is, divided her chips among all players and retreated to her true home, the baby grand piano. It meant having to put on her coat and gloves, even after we resident furniture movers pushed it closer to the heat source. I bet your last power outage didn't include a musical serenade.

Not everyone played games. Johnny made his evening rounds with the cats in the shelter and in the clinic. Chantal sat on the floor, close to the fire, and worked on the promised pajamas for Godzilla, cutting and then sewing a large piece of Christmas velour from her fabric stash. Chantal isn't an official Gregg House resident, but her fabric, makeup, costumes, and other tools of her trades do live here. She herself is present so often, either to help Dianne with taxes or travel between the music centers of Lockhart and Austin, that I wonder if her room in Austin gets any use. Fortunately, it's cheap.

Dianne pushed the sofa across the room and huddled under a blanket with her laptop. She piled the stack of spare batteries she keeps charged within arm's reach. I've seen her study for exams in the middle of a party, not surprising for someone who grew up with four younger siblings and a constant influx of aunts, uncles, and cousins. Her face intense in the ghostly light of her laptop, she barely moved except to go ask Mrs. Ly a question.

We weren't going to try to heat the gallery that night—might as well try to heat a football field—so when the logs from earlier in the day crumbled, people drifted to their sleeping quarters:

- Johnny and the male Cortez cousins in the cat shelter, always set up to have someone stay at night, if necessary
- Darryl, Zap, and Chantal (who didn't want to leave Godzilla alone, even in his new onesie) in the cat clinic with its current patients
- Mrs. Ly, Dianne's mother, and my grandparents crowded into Mrs. Ly's bedroom that shared the gallery fireplace
- The sisters (Johnny's, mine, and Dianne's) on cots in the big second floor room
- The rest of the cousins on the third floor
- Dianne in her own room, with the resident house cats and—

I stood at the top of the second-floor stairs. I'd no idea where I was going to sleep. It couldn't be that bad in my own bedroom with extra layers of socks and sweats, but I could see from where I stood that someone had bogarted my blankets, leaving only the fitted sheet. Bunking down with sisters and girl cousins seemed wrong, and I wasn't excited about either one of the cat care locations, even if they did have a generator.

Dianne shoved me in the back with her laptop. "Go."

"Where?"

"My room. I hauled in an extra cot."

That would be better than our usual practice for out-of-town gigs, renting one room with one king bed for Dianne, Chantal, and me with a rollaway bed for Johnny, who hates sleeping with anyone. We're not the wealthy rock stars who can afford to trash hotel rooms. And if you think sleeping in the same room with your ex, even on a nearby cot, would preclude sleeping, being exhausted helps.

On this, the Night of the Frozen Toes, it helped that my curvaceous ex was clad in enough winter wear to make her look like the Pillsbury Dough Boy. She topped that off with a pink-flowered flannel nightgown that covered from her neck to wrists to mid-calf (the tops of ski socks), because off-the-rack clothes are not designed for the six-foot woman. It helped that the four Very Good Kitties raised their heads and sneered at me from their perches on Dianne's bed. I would not be removing them. It helped that my sisters and her sisters were giggling in the next room. I didn't believe all that mirth was about Sophie Thi's makeup.

It helped that another bandmate thundered up the stairs with a blingified cat carrier and burst into Dianne's bedroom. Chantal announced, tears streaming down her face, that the clinic was just too cold for Godzilla, him having no fur, and she would sleep here.

As Godzilla and our Very Good Kitties protested, Dianne demanded how that could work. Chantal left the carrier on the bed and ran back downstairs. I dived for the carrier just as one pink leg with an exquisite set of curved claws escaped. I held on despite the storm inside until Dianne threw a stadium blanket over both of us. That allowed me to wiggle out, bloody. The resident cats continued their commentary. I couldn't tell who they were cheering for or against.

Chantal returned with a sleeping bag, a folded canvas, and a bag of cat supplies. Scolding us for animal cruelty, she unfolded a four-foot tall kitty playpen with a six-foot diameter. Clutching my kitty purrito while Dianne yelled at Chantal, I sat down near the head of the bed. I said nothing, there being plenty of opinions, human and feline, expressed already. Inspired by Dianne and her bag of laptop batteries, I tried to research the Texas Penal Code on my phone until Dianne diverted from Chantal to let me know how long it would be before my phone had a turn at the charger. I dabbed my wounds with a tissue instead. They weren't deep.

Gregg House's master bedroom is big enough for a party—or a king-size bed, cot, and sleeping bag in a kitty playpen, with room left over for dancing, had anyone wanted to. The distance was enough that the resident cats could ignore Godzilla confined in the playpen, where he consented to stay with Chantal in the sleeping bag. Remembering how easily he escaped the carrier, I doubted a canvas playpen could hold him, but he seemed to realize that he had the warmest, softest bed in the place. He draped himself over Chantal's head and emitted a rumbling purr that turned into a growl only when I got close enough to drop two more logs on the fire, something to be repeated throughout the night, Dianne and I taking turns.

I never got used to the phone alarm dragging me awake to face the pair of demonic eyes, glowing by the fire. It was worse when he opened his mouth into a smile, fangs gleaming. I was glad my cot was beside Dianne's makeshift altar on her nightstand, where I could smell the aroma of the Guadalupe rosewood rosary her grandmother gave her for her confirmation. Take that, vampire cat.

I intended to be noble and not say a word about my cot. Though too short for my six-foot-three frame, it did have some padding, at least as thick as a processed cheese slice. The standard-issue blanket was one of those space-age thin foil ones that claimed to be as warm as a regular model. That might be true. Maybe no blanket sold in Texas would be effective on a night like this. I had a chance to test that theory as I scrunched up under it.

Dianne turned off all her devices and wiggled across her bed closer to me. She draped half of her blankets over me, making my life instantly better. Her gardenia perfume mixed with the rosary's soapy rosewood scent.

Also, I was warmer.

I still had trouble sleeping in the pure silence. Life in small-town Beauchamp is quiet, but it was spooky with absolutely no traffic or house noise beyond a popping log. Somewhere around 4:00 A.M., the central heating system kicked in again. All the humans in the room sighed in relief. Dianne rolled over, deep in sleep, and her arm fell over me. Figuring I had the same plausible deniability of continued slumber, I moved until my hand touched hers. Inhaling gardenia and rosewood anew, I thought about many things, including putting another log on the fire, but in the end, I just fell into a deep sleep for the first time that night.

CHAPTER 17

I opened my sleep-crusted eyes to the sun sneaking around the corners of the blackout shades. Dianne's bed is in the second-floor turret and so surrounded by windows. I yawned and wondered if I should interfere with the rumble the growling kittens were planning, when Dianne emerged from her closet-dressing room and scooped up silky gold Nevada from the group surrounding the playpen.

She wore full business drag, gray wool suit and coat. The cat hair lint roller in one hand and the squirming cat tucked under her other arm spoiled the image of the Power Latina, ready to rule government or corporation, but they helped me with the shock. I couldn't remember the last time I saw La Chica Fuerte.

She spoke in a husky whisper, out of courtesy for our slumbering roommate. "You awake, JD? Don't count me for breakfast. I'm off to deliver gingerbread houses, but I'll put our cats out of the room. Chantal's sound asleep, of course, and if she can sleep with a cat on her head and her feet in its litter box, more power to her."

I yawned. "Any luck with the research?"

Her lips curled into a smile packed with threats that I wouldn't want aimed at me. "Oh yes. I was bound to find something in twenty years. Now to confirm. No connection with European industry though, everything very local, depending on how you define local. I finished the spreadsheet of where everybody was and who they saw. A big lot of nothing. I opened up the permissions to you and Johnny. Would you send it Alejandro?"

"Probably not."

"What? I promised him. You promised him."

"Because I'm representing everybody on that list, and I don't want to hand the police possibly incriminating evidence."

"You said you couldn't represent everybody."

"But for now I am. Officer Al can get that information by interviewing everybody."

"Except you've told them not to say anything. JD, it's in our best interests to get along with the police, and believe me, nobody said, 'Oh look, there goes a murderer, off to murder someone.'" Her voice didn't get louder, but the hisses got sharper.

"Dianne, almost twenty of those witnesses are your family. Can you imagine what your mother would say if your work helped get any of them charged with murder?"

Dianne turned pale, turning her makeup orange in contrast. "¡Madre de Dios! JD, yesterday we told them that we were going to prove that they didn't murder anyone. And now you don't want to give that proof to the police?"

"I don't know what it proves—I haven't seen it."

"I know my sisters and cousins would never murder anyone. You don't sound as sure about your sisters. Or Johnny's."

I let silence lie between us like roadkill until she dropped her furious gaze. "I haven't been doing this lawyer thing long compared to, say, my grandfather and father, but I've done it long enough to be convinced that anyone could do anything if sufficiently provoked. I've heard several compelling reasons for murder, and that's only what people were willing to tell me. And I'm worried about what the data and photos might unintentionally show or what could be twisted into something harmful. I want to hear whether Johnny spots any patterns or problems."

"And then you'll turn it over to Officer Alejandro?"

"Then I'll do what's best for my clients."

Dianne took a deep breath and cursed me out in Spanish, but absolutely silently, just moving her lips, as she snatched up the rest of the Very Good Kitties. I didn't catch all of it, but I got the gist.

Arms full of kittens, all calling one last "coulda-woulda-shoulda," she sashayed from the room. I swung my legs out of bed with a groan. On normal days, Dianne and Johnny would have risen at yawn o'clock for their morning run, and I would have scribbled poetry in my journal before descending to the kitchen to prepare breakfast.

Nothing was normal, but I was betting everyone would still congregate at the dining table, waiting for me to produce something.

Everyone agrees I'm useless as a cook except for breakfast, but my repertoire isn't large: pancakes or waffles, eggs scrambled or fried, bacon or sausage, and whatever fruit lurks in the fridge—or in Dad's Pittman & Davis boxes. It seems to satisfy people, and of course they're welcome to cook for themselves.

But they don't ever go to that extreme. Mrs. Cortez and the grandparents were gathered around the table, sipping their favorite beverage and nibbling on party leftovers. I mumbled a good morning and started cracking eggs.

For some reason, Dianne's remark about twenty years stuck with me. Twenty years kept coming up. Did it mean something? Should I scramble twenty eggs? That sounded right. I rummaged through the pantry for Johnny's industrial-sized pans and turned on the griddle. I grabbed a bag of bacon from the freezer—Dianne and I keep bags of meat ready to supplement Johnny's vegetarian cuisine.

I could see the Brandon house from the window. I sent a dollop of sympathy, wincing at memories of the days after my mother died. I could promise the Brandons that many more dreadful mornings lay ahead.

What had the last twenty years done for them or to them? Miss Leigh slid gracefully into her elder years, despite her husband's death and her grown children moving out of state. She still had her friends and her church. Claire raised a daughter, established a business, and bloomed into a reinvented self, unrecognizable to the girl she had been. Melanie grasped the husband and life she thought she wanted, but I'd never noticed that they or the resulting four children brought her joy. I wondered if she liked children or had just been taught that until she never questioned it. As for her husband, whatever she felt or thought she felt about him was now irrelevant, though bound to leave a hole in her life after twenty years.

Twenty years again. Twenty years.

I wondered how much of a financial hole Lem's absence would leave. I doubted his name was among the Young Millionaires; farmers tend not to be. From my kitchen window, I could see the huge Pacifica SUV in the driveway, the one Miss Leigh gave Melanie last year. Miss Leigh was generous, but she wouldn't have given her daughter such a car just for fun.

I turned the mass of scrambled eggs into a warming tray and slapped another round of pancakes on the griddle. As they sizzled, I pulled out my phone to send a text to the Brandons. I offered to fix breakfast, because we hadn't yet sent over the customary casserole or pound cake (not required by Southern law, just Southern courtesy, which is more compelling).

I set out enough pancakes, eggs, and bacon to feed a starving country and told the bleary-eyed crew at the table they were on their own. I then poured the remaining pancake batter into a bottle, grabbed another bag of bacon, and bundled myself up enough to walk across the street without freezing. To get myself out of everybody's bad books and to save all the people who claimed to be my clients, I needed to find the murderer. Then our photos and testimony would be supporting, not incriminating, evidence.

Claire met me at the side door. I told her I wanted to talk to her sister.

Claire glanced over her shoulder at Melanie, slumped down in her chair at the kitchen table. "I'll put on a movie, and the kids can eat in front of the TV. Mother ate a chocolate before bed last night, so she's still asleep."

She lowered her voice even more. "Melanie just heard that Lem was murdered, stabbed, but not all the way into the heart, several hours before he died. That's why he could walk around for a while, until finally it tore open while he was walking and why there's no clues from where he died. That's not where he was stabbed. The kids don't know yet."

The kids fled to the living room as soon as they grasped the program, and Claire headed off the inevitable fight over a movie by not asking them, just queuing up the latest *Toy Story*, which they all abused in perfect agreement. They shut up and munched as soon as they had food in front of them.

Taking over the cooking area, I was left to converse with Melanie with a Pixar accompaniment. Pixar spoke in longer sentences than she did. More intelligibly too. Frying aromas filled the kitchen, a combination of batter and bacon, but they didn't loosen her tongue like I'd hoped.

I made one more stab at condolences as I delivered her plate. "I'm so sorry this happened on Lem's first trip back to Beauchamp in so many years. I hope he got to do some of the things he was looking forward to."

Melanie crunched a slice of bacon, because first things first. "I don't know. Maybe? But Guy's dead too, so I don't know." Her voice broke, but another slice of bacon helped. With her full attention, she applied butter and syrup to the pancakes, rendering them into pancake soup.

"I remember seeing them laughing together at the party. At least they had a few happy minutes together."

I had no idea who would eat what I was cooking now, but it seemed important to keep going, to stand at the stove behind her. As though on cue, three teenage boys called for seconds. I should have known, having been one. I ignored their mother's shaking shoulders as I delivered the second course, same as the first, to the living room.

Melanie sobbed, "I don't know what to do now. Lem said he had to come back because he and Guy and Doug made an investment that was supposed to mature in twenty years. Is that the word? *Mature*? I don't know anything about investments. But they all had to be here to collect. Can he still collect if he's dead? I don't know anything about it, so I can't look. I'd ask Doug, but the police took Lem's phone and I don't have his friends' numbers."

Investment. What kind of investment could teenagers have made twenty years ago? Twenty years—I had it. I consulted the source of all knowledge (my phone) to be sure, but now I knew for sure what *20 30.02* meant, and why Guy Randall and Lem Quiston died.

CHAPTER 18

I flipped a few more pancakes and left them and the remains of the bacon bag as I zoomed back home. A different, younger crew now held court at the table, young women picking at food they claimed they never ate but visibly enjoying it. The Cortez contingent was singing the praises of their new makeup. Merry was picking through Sophie Thi's samples.

Cherry said to Sophie Thi, "But nobody's whiter than my family, so if these products are made for BIPOC, they wouldn't be good for us."

"That's a common fallacy," Sophie Thi assured her. "You see, my company understands skin color. Nobody's white, and white people are all shades of beige, coral, and pink. Most makeup makes them look like corpses, whereas my products are designed to bring out those undertones. I've got this awesome idea. You put on your makeup, and I'll do Merry's, so you can see the difference. Twins! That's ideal for a test."

They were not interested in me, but I raised my voice anyway, "Great idea. Have you seen Johnny?"

It was almost a universal Nope, but someone thought she'd seen Johnny emerge from the cat shelter and go somewhere in his truck.

"Dianne?" I asked as I made a call to the police. Officer Alejandro Quintanilla-Villanueva was not available.

They all agreed Dianne was still out delivering gingerbread houses to their original makers.

"She looked like somebody in Congress," Cherry said, to a chorus of agreement.

I tried my stern elder brother voice. "And you're also delivering houses, remember? If you aren't, you're cleaning the kitchen and preparing for the concert tonight." I'm sure they heard me as they debated Dianne's sartorial choices and a blush shade for Merry.

The food tables were still in place (because the easiest way to get people to come to something is to promise free food), but they were still covered in gingerbread houses, bagged with their destination taped to the bag. They reminded me of a cookie-based mobile home repo auction. On the furthest table, between the Christmas tree and the clinic door, stood five sad houses marked only with a question mark, as though nobody knew where they belonged. They gave me an idea.

Chantal had been afraid that no one would make anything for our gingerbread house display. Since she doesn't live here full time, she's not aware of how Darryl has the whole town trained to participate in whatever nuttiness we dream up. Ask me about High Holy Days. So she badgered us all into making houses, to be sure that we had some to display. They weren't needed, but they were there, ready to be stomped by Monster Cat Godzilla, and our repair team lovingly put them back together, even though they ranked with the shabbiest efforts. I grabbed one at random and headed for the door.

Chantal, cat in arms, staggered down the stairs. "JD, I want to rehearse with you. The Handel."

I turned the back doorknob. "You won't be conscious for another half hour or in singing voice for an hour. We'll rehearse when I get back. Won't be long. I'm just taking this house to Doug Severn."

Chantal clutched Godzilla close so she could run down the last few steps. "That's not even his cookie house. JD, listen."

I didn't.

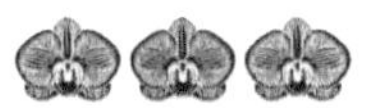

I took my car for the sole purpose of driving a block away from the sound of Chantal's voice—she really shouldn't raise it like that on performance day. I checked my phone maps to make sure I had the right address. I looked at the overhead and street views too. Across the street from the mayor's house, people said.

That was indeed true. The average number of walls in Beauchamp houses is less than four, and total roof coverage reached a maximum 80% when the wind wasn't blowing. Dianne calculated that while we were munching on fried spring rolls in the Happy Family Asian restaurant a few weeks ago. If Dianne has no numbers to fiddle with, she finds some.

The mayor's house sprawled over two lots, a long brick ranch stylish in the last century. A wide arc of a driveway followed the line of the house to destroy most of the lawn. Northwest of that stood another house, also covering two lots, but leaving more yard space because of its two stories. It needed the yard space for the pool and party patio in the back.

The house must have been built in the last twenty years. It sported a boxy, brutal floor plan with floor-to-ceiling windows, solar panels on a sloped tiled roof, and a facade of irregular brown-speckled Texas stone. Rattlesnake stone, it's called, appropriate for the occasion.

The doorbell rang in cavernous tones, into the next county, it sounded like. I looked as pleasant and dumb as possible for the security camera while I wondered what I'd do if no one answered. Before I figured that out, the door opened.

I recognized the man from Saturday's open house. Just as his house was a bit richer than its neighbors, his clothes were a notch better than mine, teeth whiter, hair blonder (even styled). If they didn't convince me of my inferiority, no doubt he had more weapons in his arsenal.

That was true. I saw a literal arsenal on the jagged stone wall behind him as I gave my patter speech about the stupid gingerbread house. Texans like their native stone inside the house too, and this limestone was white, the better to show off a museum-quality collection of stabby weapons from across the ages: swords, spears, knives, things I couldn't identify. They all ended in sharp points, some of them multiple sharp points.

I pushed forward as though he'd invited me in, using the gingerbread house as a battering ram. Something in the corner of my eye, something that didn't belong, by the chairs and side tables, caught my attention, but I shrugged it off in my focus on the display of killing tools. "Hey! Those are fantastic. I'm fascinated with weapons."

My usual fascination with weapons is in calculating how far away I can remove myself. Today I wondered if my SAT and LSAT scores were wrong, because I was moving toward dangerous weapons instead of away. I could have been back in my car in ten seconds, since I'd pulled up to the door rather than park in the large concrete space to the east, for party parking or party spillover from the back. Is this where the cool kids go on New Year's? No one at Gregg House was invited. I didn't mind.

He scowled as my clueless persona tromped into the sunken living room to examine the Wall of Weapons on the far side of the room. The stone eventually turned into a fireplace, but the weapons drew the eye. Just me, him, and a room full of weapons.

From a far-away part of the house, I could hear a voice or voices, not loud or distinct enough to identify people or words. Were they people in a conversation? In a movie? The news? More importantly, if I yelled, would they run to help me, or Doug? Or not at all?

"Mind if I take some photos? These are amazing." I didn't wait for permission—fortunate, because he didn't give it.

"I'd rather you didn't. I'd rather not have it known what's in my collection. Not good for security." He tacked a smile over his scowl, and the upturned lips looked odd under the deep, dead eyes.

As he moved closer, blocking my way to the door, I stepped back, exclaiming as I examined the weapons, trying to determine which ones were fastened to the wall and which I could grab if necessary.

Lately people talk a lot about smiles: the full-on, eye crinkling, soul-bubbling laugh-smile called Duchenne, like Dianne when the numbers balance. There's the social smile, something Johnny has practiced for public interaction, a pleasant, mouth-curving expression designed to stop people from asking "What's wrong?" And then there's the smiles made from different Potato Head sets, the evil eyes a stark contrast over mouth and teeth that haven't mastered the instructions.

That's what I saw on Doug Severn. The smile to stay away from.

But I didn't. "You're right—not good for security. Sorry! We were just talking about that this weekend. Mrs. Ly had her family jewelry stolen before she could get it secured, because someone knew she had it." I pretended to delete the photos as I set the phone to record before shoving it in my pocket.

I thought I saw the flicker of a snake's tongue, which suited his features better than the smile debacle.

I blithered on. "It must be twenty years now. Sorry about the loss of your friends. What are the odds? Two friends die the same day, after being apart for twenty years."

He held himself perfectly still, but his eyes burned. "Very sad. That crazy Brandon woman must have done it. I've told the police what I know about her."

"Which one?" I asked, disinterested.

He started. "Claire. The one that sells pot brownies. I could tell you things about her. I've asked the police for protection."

"Oh. I meant which death."

He started. "Guy, of course. Lem wasn't murdered, was he? I mean, Claire probably drove him into a heart attack. She's like that."

I pretended confusion. "Wasn't he married to Melanie? It's been years since he was in the same state as Claire."

He held up his hands. "Just what I heard. The gossip machine is in full throttle."

"That's true. I heard that Lem might have been murdered the same way as the Empress Elisabeth."

"What does that mean? He wasn't murdered, was he?"

I still had no idea. "I don't know. I'm not a historian or the medical examiner. People will say anything, won't they? Like about Mrs. Ly's jewelry. I hear they've found new evidence to reopen the case. I hope so. It was such a shame to have it stolen after her family brought it with them when they escaped the Nazis."

If Doug was a snake, his rattles would be mariachi level and his head raised to strike. He edged toward the wall. The only way this case made sense was if you connected it with crimes that started twenty years ago in Gregg House.

I stepped away from him, like we were in a slow circle dance. "You must have been a kid then. Do you remember it? The theft wasn't discovered until much later, but now they have a good idea when it took place, and they can narrow down the suspect list. Found some of the jewelry too."

In a sudden movement, he grabbed a stiletto from the wall. "You might be interested in this one."

Instead of holding it out to show me, he pulled back his arm in a throwing position. I jumped out of range. At the same time, the front door crashed open, and Johnny plowed through, unstoppable.

I jumped between them. "It is not a good day for anybody to die!"

Johnny stumbled sideways so as not to run into me, revealing Dianne in the doorway behind him as she raised the gun in her hand. He whispered a warning, and I caught sight of a blade coming at my back. Stony-faced, Dianne fired.

CHAPTER 19

Everyone jumped when the bullet shattered a brick to the left of his knee. He screamed as the rock fuselage struck him. I was glad I was further away—even gladder that he dropped the stiletto. I lunged and made a wide sweep with my leg that would have earned me a place with a professional soccer team or ballet company. The gleaming blade spun away, stopping when Johnny put his foot on it.

Dianne sighed and jerked her chin toward the door in a message to Johnny and me. "I need practice. I was aiming at the brick next to it, the one with the edge sticking out more than the others. No, the one below that. But holidays, you know? So much to do. Still, I hope you're convinced that I can hit close to what I aim at, though no guarantees. If I aim to wound, it might be worse."

I glided in slo-mo towards the door. When I reached Johnny, he stooped and retrieved the captured weapon with one of the crime-scene gloves he carries. We continued our waltz out the front door with Dianne covering us.

"Johnny, you drive Dianne's car," I force-whispered as I jumped into my Hyundai Sonata. I forgot to scrunch down and banged my head on the ceiling.

Nodding, Johnny took the driver's seat of her little Honda and started it. We all have keys to each other's cars, but only Johnny carries all of them. He mouthed "police station" as he held up the stiletto, still wrapped in his glove.

Dianne backed out of the house and snapped, "Hands up behind your head. Count to ninety-seven." She slammed the door shut in lock mode. She sank into my passenger seat, gun pointed at the door.

"Why?" she and I demanded in chorus.

"Same reason railroads send a new crew after a train runs over someone on the track," I answered, stomping the accelerator. Gravel crunched and flew as we sped in the opposite direction from Johnny. Doug couldn't come after both of us. "Why ninety-seven?"

"Largest prime number under a hundred," she replied, voice terse. She was shaking, but not from the cold. That didn't stop her from scolding, flopping back and forth between her two native languages. "¿Porque, pendejo, porque? Why did you go to Doug's house alone? Fue una estupidez. I met with the town's bankers this morning, and the police can get a warrant to look at Doug's twenty years of unexplained wealth."

I glanced in the rearview mirror. No one behind me. Yet. I turned left at random. "I didn't know that, but I did have an idea what happened to the jewelry and why Lem and Guy were killed—why Doug killed them."

Dianne didn't reply. I glanced at her, rigid, lips pursed, arms clutching her abdomen.

"Pull over," she demanded.

I did after turning right, a block from the highway. She threw open the door and heaved her breakfast into the ditch. I reached over to hold her hair out of the spew. I stroked the ends. I knew she didn't want to be touched, not with fire ants running up and down every nerve.

"S'all right," I murmured as I looked out the back window. I did this on her twenty-first birthday after the celebration of all the legal liquor she could drink. Or rather, couldn't. I glanced down the side street. Also that time she had the flu. I craned my neck to look in the opposite direction. Maybe one more in the last decade? Still no one.

She sagged back in the seat and shut her eyes. I tossed paper napkins from local restaurants her way and took off before she finished shutting the door.

She made half-hearted efforts at clean up while I got on the highway and mulled over where to go next. Not home. I didn't want to lead Doug there.

She murmured in a thread of a voice. "Mi tío Pedro, when he taught me to shoot, said he hoped I'd never shoot anything except a target, but if I had to protect myself or someone else, he wanted to be sure I'd never hesitate."

"The military tío?"

"Yes. I've never shot at anybody before. Usually a crazy Latina with a gun makes people back off."

"As someone else, I'm grateful to him and you. You did shoot at a brick, or does that count?"

She opened one eye and shut it again. "No, because if he hadn't stopped, he would have taken the next bullet, I promise. Where are we going?"

"Away, where Doug won't find us if he gives chase. Send a text to everybody at the house and tell them to watch out for him. He really does know where we live."

She pulled out her phone, but said, "Not for a while, unless he calls a rideshare. Even then, it takes thirty minutes to get a driver to Beauchamp."

"How do you figure? He might have gone after Johnny, but he'll change his mind when he sees the police station."

"Because we didn't burst in as soon as we got to his house, and while Johnny kept watch, I disabled his cars. Mi tío Abejundio taught me many ways to put a car out of commission. I was glad for the chance to practice them. He's the one who owns a garage—"

"Chop-shop?"

"That ladrón, yes."

"A toast to you and Tío Abejundio."

I drove to the nearest C-store on the highway. While I paid for a Diet Pepsi, a bottle of water, and coffee, she nipped out of the car to throw away the wad of napkins. I might have seen the edge of her gray leather gloves in the mess, but I wasn't sure enough to testify, if anyone asked. Her hands wouldn't show that she'd fired a gun, no powder burns. Or maybe the gloves were covered in vomit. I studied the lottery tickets to give her more time to settle back into the car.

Someone needed to give Dianne a nice pair of gray leather gloves for Christmas. Since I already had something for her, I thought I'd tell her mother, who acted as Christmas Central for the family. Every year Dianne gets emails and texts from her mother saying, "Your father needs—" "Lourdes wants—" "The family's chipping in for a car for Cousin Pilar." Conchita Cortez would jump on gloves like the Very Good Kitties on a tuna pizza.

As I settled in the car, Dianne tossed back a big slug of Pepsi, savoring it with a ghost of a smile.

Our phones pinged us at the same time. Johnny's text said that he found Officer Al at our home, interviewing Claire Brandon about Doug's accusations. In my absence, my grandfather was representing her. Officer Al was glad to wrap up that interview and look at Johnny's possible evidence.

After another soothing drink, Dianne leaned back and closed her eyes. "The medical examiner called Johnny this morning. He said that Lem was stabbed with something slim and sharp."

"Like that stiletto? It was nice and shiny, like it was just cleaned."

"Could be." Dianne belted back another swig and held it in her mouth while the bubbles fizzed. "The wound didn't go all the way into his heart. His moving around tore it the rest of the way."

That's what I heard from Claire. "Is that how Empress Elisabeth died?"

"Similar, according to Johnny. No one, even her, knew she'd been stabbed at first. She fell down or fainted and then got up and went about her day until she suddenly died. It sounds like Lem did the same."

"Did the security footage and the alibi spreadsheet show anything useful?" I sipped the coffee, hot but horrible. I suspected it was yesterday's leftovers. If not, a seriously incompetent barista made it, which you'd expect at a highway C-store. But "hot" outweighed all other considerations for me on a morning like this.

"Johnny glanced at the spreadsheet and said the footage confirmed what people said, that Guy, Lem, and Doug left at different times, about fifteen minutes apart. Our cameras showed only directly behind the house, by the shelter, not all the way to the back fence, behind the row of apartments. I'm guessing they set up a meeting that they didn't want anyone to notice."

"And Doug killed Guy and a few minutes later stabbed Lem. Maybe he fell down, and Doug ran off to establish his alibi, thinking Lem was done for. But he wasn't, and he was able to get back to the house. He looked awful at my all-call legal meeting, but I put it down to the shock of his friend's death." I started the car to let the heater catch up.

"*Friend* isn't the word we want for people who rob an elderly lady and then kill each other to keep the proceeds. I'm not sure what happened in the twenty years after the theft."

"I think I do. They stole the jewelry they found in Mrs. Ly's house. She didn't discover it right away, which helped them. They decided to wait until the statute of limitations ran out. The most that could be for burglary is twenty years, as described in Section 30.02 of the Texas Penal Code. I bet that was Doug's idea, since he ended up with the jewelry. They should have had legal advice, but that's hard to get when you're planning a crime." I steeled myself for another sip of hot sludge.

"Twenty years!"

"Indeed, like on the slip of paper in Lem's pocket. The twenty years having run out, Guy and Lem wanted their share, now that they were safe and their 'investment' had 'matured,' as Lem told Melanie. Only Doug spent it, probably cutting the jewelry into its component stones so that he could sell them gradually and they would be less likely to be traced. Rather than tell his friends or try to gather enough cash to buy them off, he killed them."

"No, *friends* is not the word we want here." Dianne finished her drink and closed her eyes for a moment to remember the ecstasy. "Don't we have to pick up our order for Mama Ana's tamales?"

I put the car in gear. "I can take you home first."

"I don't want to go home. Everyone's in full event-prep mode for the concert tonight—or should be, and I'll have to kick them into gear, if they're not."

"Tonight you're a performer. No reason you can't go to your room and lie down for a while, not with your mother, sisters, cousins, Darryl, and Chantal on hand."

"Then I'd have listen to 'Shhh, Dianne's resting,' 'Leave Dianne alone so she can sleep,' and worst of all: 'We'll figure it out. Don't bother Dianne.' Just let me have a few minutes when I don't have to do or say anything."

I was already pulling into the parking lot where Mama Ana parks her food truck. She wasn't on duty, and her daughter was grouchy for having to open up at all today, despite the whole town having declared itself unable to move for the snow, now mostly melted from the roads. But somebody had to come in because they had this big order for the Black Orchids. I don't know though to hear her tell it, she had taken her life into her hands to toddle a half-mile down the street to open the stand just for us, when obviously they'd have no lunch business on a snow day.

She cheered up when I bought the rest of her product for Gregg House's lunch. A few customers did wander in, and we shared our haul with them. She had the truck closed for business before my tires crunched through the gravel parking lot.

Back at the house, I reveled in being swarmed by twenty nubile young women, even if they were grabbing tamales and tacos instead of fawning over me. Chantal ended the fantasy when she grabbed the bags from me to sling the lunch food on the table and the concert food into the fridge. She then grabbed my arm and pulled me toward the piano.

"I swear, JD, we are rehearsing now, before the artists arrive. I've been warming up ever since you left. The cellist from the string trio offered to play continuo on the Handel. We'll rehearse with her later. I want the rest of our set perfect before then."

"Lunch first?" I looked longingly at the bags on the table getting flatter.

"No." She jumped up to push down on my shoulder. I sank onto the piano bench with a sigh but no tamale.

Johnny banged through the clinic door. "JD, come with me. There's been a death at the Severn house."

"Lunch first?"

"Bring it with you."

I zoomed in to snatch the last two tamales, beating out other hands on the same mission. But one hand was my grandmother's, and her expression was so saintly and sad that I gave them to her.

CHAPTER 20

Chantal's curses sped us on our way, a short way past downtown Beauchamp to the good block in town, if you didn't count Gregg House. Johnny didn't know any more than he'd already said. I knew we'd left Doug alive, but I had to keep telling myself that.

Officer Al, simmering, waited for us at the door, as we donned crime scene booties and gloves. I received stony silence in response to my greeting. I took a deep breath and tensed as we entered the weaponry room. A quick glance relieved my fears but gave me a shock. No crime scene here, but pieces of the puzzle fell together.

I'd met the slender, honey-haired woman scrunched in the uncomfortably modern chair.

I tried to make introductions. "Johnny, this is Ms.—I didn't catch your name. She came to see Godzilla yesterday, but you weren't at home. This is Dr. Johnny Ly, Assistant Justice of the Peace."

"Anelia Severn," she croaked, voice raw. She didn't offer to shake hands, her arms being folded tightly across her chest, but she lifted her head to look at us. A new bruise was spreading over one cheek, with two thumb marks on her neck.

Her chair sat next to the table by the door, the one I'd glimpsed earlier. I blinked at a photo in a gleaming frame. Now I knew what struck me as out of place. The photo showed Anelia on a happier day snuggled her cheek against Godzilla's. He didn't look as fierce as he did in our house, almost content, though the blue eyes still glared. With her glorious golden hair and violet eyes radiating nobility, Anelia looked like a candidate for my Mrs. Robinson, if only the circumstances had been right. "He's yours, isn't he? Godzilla?"

"You can look at cat photos another time. The JP has a job to do," growled Officer Al, belligerent. He glared a challenge at Johnny. "I'm thinking it's suicide."

Not something I wanted to hear (and imagine), and the wife didn't either, from her expression.

"Yes. With my gun," she whispered. She waved to the wall of sharp-pointed things, exposing an arm with fresh and healed scratches. "He preferred knives and such, but not for—not for what he did. He knew where I kept it. You'll find my prints on it too, of course. He hit me—I can't exactly remember everything. He thought I had money, and he wanted it. We'd been fighting for days. Today he grabbed my gun. We struggled for it, and then he knocked me down and ran in the den. I called 911 when I heard the shot."

Fighting meant he'd been hitting her for days, judging by the older wounds exposed every time she moved.

"I'm sorry for your loss," I burbled in confusion. I couldn't be too sorry that her torture had ended. Her physical torture anyway.

She ducked her head in acknowledgement and turned her body away from the crime scene room, towards the window. Her blouse shifted, revealing the edge of a nasty green bruise on her shoulder.

After one nod of condolence to Anelia Severn, Johnny followed Officer Al into the next room. Not being fond of crime scenes, I stayed behind.

"What's Godzilla's real name?" I asked, not wanting to hear the proceedings in the next room before I had to.

"Sir Percival Nofurr," she said, tilting her head back to look at me. The rich waves of hair fell back from her face to reveal careful makeup at her left temple, perhaps to cover another bruise. "I expect he likes Godzilla better. Why did you call him that?"

"It seemed natural after he wrecked the gingerbread house village. We first saw him swinging on a hanging flower basket on the front porch. He leapt from one to the other, and when we went out to see what was happening, he darted into the house. Our cats had escaped their confinement, and they chased each other up and down the Great Hall, right through the houses."

A slight smile danced on her lips. "That sounds just like him. He likes to swing on my porch ferns and tear them up. I have to replace them every few months."

"Later we found his carrier on the clinic porch. Did you put him there? The security camera footage wasn't clear, but it did show him scrambling from the carrier."

The smile turned into fury. "My husband did. He told me he got rid of Percy. I hoped he'd escaped, because Doug was stupid enough to put him in that carrier that's more decorative than secure. Percy's been able to escape that one since he was a kitten. But that's Doug for you. When I wanted a kitten, he bought one for my birthday that looked like a pink naked bat, complete with a satin bed and carrier. I was horrified, which made Doug laugh, but it was a kitten, a scared kitten, and I felt I had to love him, and then I did, to the point where I didn't understand why people laughed at him. Doug liked to show him to his friends as a joke."

"I think I understand why you didn't claim him."

She covered her eyes. "I saw the poster. I saw the TikTok. My first thought was to run get him. Then—that's why I asked what you were going to do with him."

"Beauchamp is a no-kill city," said Johnny.

Both she and I started; we hadn't heard him re-enter the room. I glanced at my watch. It takes Johnny hours to process a crime scene. He couldn't possibly be through already.

Anelia leaned forward, yearning. "I need to go to the police station and give my statement. May I come visit Percy—Godzilla—afterwards?"

Johnny frowned. "Yes."

"And we've got a concert this evening too, if you'd like to stay," I added, to help the cause.

Johnny took a stance like the sword-wielding angel at the Garden of Eden's gate. "I'd already decided not to return Godzilla to his previous home. I don't think he was treated well."

Anelia's eyes filled with tears. "I suspect that's true. Doug never did anything to him in front of me, but Percy either avoided Doug or attacked him and ran off."

In typical neutral tones, Johnny remarked, "I had to take my assistant to the emergency room after Percy bit him. He reacts violently to being around men, and cat bites are dangerous."

She wept into her hands. "I should have found him another home. I know what Doug is. Was."

"Condolences on your loss, Mrs. Severn." Officer Al's voice was wry, one point away from outright sarcasm. "Johnny, could we finish processing this case before you move on to your duties as Assistant Animal Control Officer?"

"Certainly, Officer. I don't see any reason to disagree with your conclusion of suicide."

Al's jaw dropped, just like mine. I snapped it shut.

"You don't?" asked Al, as gobsmacked as I was.

"No," replied Johnny, laconic as always.

"That's that, then," I declared. "We might as well go, if you don't want to call for an autopsy, a toxicology report, and the rest of it."

"No need for any of that, not that I can see," Johnny confirmed as he turned to Mrs. Severn. "I would like to ask whether your husband had any antique jewelry."

"Here we go," muttered Officer Al.

Anelia nodded, puzzled. "We fought about it last week. When we got married, he gave me two diamond bracelets and a ruby necklace as a present. He said they had been in his family for generations."

Sorrowful, she turned away to gaze at their framed wedding invitation on the same table with Godzilla's photo. I squinted to read the date, some eight years ago, as I handed her my phone. "Does your jewelry look anything like this ring?"

"Yes, it matches the bracelets. He said the ring had been lost, that he wished he could give it to me as an engagement ring. He gave me a modern one instead." She spread her fingers wide, an unconscious movement that emphasized the lack of jewelry, except for a thin silver band on her left hand.

Face blank as a snowbank, Johnny asked, "What did you fight about last week?"

"He wanted the jewelry back." She held up her left hand to show us. "He'd already taken my engagement ring when he needed money for—I don't know what. He never said. After that, I put anything that I valued in a safe deposit box, in my name only. I—I've been planning to leave him for some time. I put aside everything I could for that day. I never told him, of course, and last week he tore up the house looking for the bracelets and necklace. He said he owed his friends money, that he had to pay them this weekend. Do you think he killed them? I was terrified when I heard they died."

"I do think so," Johnny agreed. "But that's just my opinion, not part of my duties as Assistant Justice of the Peace. They both were murdered, one possibly with a weapon from that wall. As for why, I believe the investigation will show that Doug and his friends stole my family's jewelry twenty years ago, jewelry that was in our family for generations, brought to this country when my ancestors escaped the Holocaust. Doug seems to have been the only one who used the proceeds, establishing his business, building this house, wooing his wife, buying her an expensive kitten when so many are waiting to be rescued." His voice turned ominous, and it took him some seconds to recover. Doug should be glad he's dead. Johnny nodded to Officer Al. "Talk to Dianne about getting a subpoena for his banking records. She's also compiled a spreadsheet of our household's activities and observations of Doug, Guy, and Lem at Saturday's open house."

Officer Al exploded, "Why didn't you give me this before?"

"We didn't have it before. Dianne couldn't talk to her banking contacts until this morning, and it took some time to gather and enter the data, especially with yesterday's power outage. The patterns weren't evident until we had all the data in one place."

"You've obstructed every step of these investigations!"

Johnny held up a hand. "I haven't obstructed, but I admit I haven't participated. Surely you can see why. These men harmed my family. How could I investigate? If it were your family involved, you'd hand the case to another officer. As it is, Dianne's efforts can help close the cases. The only thing I don't know is why Guy and Lem waited twenty years to ask for their share, but maybe it's not critical information. You won't be going to trial."

I cleared my throat. "I have that one. The paper in Lem's pocket that read *20 30.02*? He took notes: *30.02* refers to the Texas Penal Code section that specifies twenty years as the longest statute of limitations for burglary. It looks like the plan was for Doug to hold the goods for them all until the statute of limitations expired, when they would split the profits. Only Doug didn't wait. I suspect he had the jewelry chopped into its stones and sold those to keep him off the insurance company's and law enforcement's radar. He didn't move much at any one time. But after twenty years, he no longer had anything to give his partners."

"Then he killed them," finished Johnny. "And then killed himself, full of remorse. That or he saw the investigation closing in on him."

Anelia stared at her clenched hands.

CHAPTER 21

Chantal's dulcet tones struck us as we entered the house. "JD, you get over to the piano right now and rehearse with me."

I did, but I protested, "We've got hours yet."

Godzilla lay curled in a ball on the lid, daring me to raise it. His pink skin glowed in the afternoon sun that dared to creep through the gauzy curtains. I decided I didn't need the lid up.

"And the other musicians will be here. Some are here already. Two Met auditions finalists, a Tchaikovsky competitor, and I don't know what all."

That did make me sick to my stomach. I hadn't had piano lessons since my senior year in high school, never had voice lessons, unless you count ten years of Chantal's haranguing, and I was going to stand up (or sit on a piano bench) with an ABBA tribute band and pretend I could make music.

What amazed me was that Chantal felt the same way, and she at least had a bachelor's degree in music (a double major with accountancy so she could get a real job). I'd heard her in recitals, concerts, opera, gospel brunches, churches, and bars ranging from dives to upper crust salons, and always and everywhere she exuded the confidence that she had a right to be there and everyone would be glad to hear her, an attitude we absorbed when we performed with her. Now she was as ashen as her Mississippi-mud colored skin would allow, her eyes dilated and fearful.

"JD, they're going to be here any minute, and I can't bear to practice in front of them. And everybody will need a turn at the piano."

People really do wring their hands, I noted as I raised the keyboard cover. Godzilla shifted to the far end of the piano and glared at me.

I returned the glare. "Shut up and sing."

She gulped a breath and let forth the "Rejoice" aria from Handel's *Messiah*, something from her junior recital that she'd performed a million times since, it being a holiday favorite in churches. She could and probably did sing it in her sleep. She does sing in her sleep—I assume that noise is singing—but never anything I recognize.

The point is, she didn't need to rehearse that piece. She gasped through it in half-voice, like she was drowning.

I was worried. After her last croak, a note truncated to a tenth of what the composer wrote, I said, "Why don't we warm up on something? The bell song, maybe?"

She took a deep breath and launched into the Ukrainian song, "Carol of the Bells," which sounded odd with her in the rafters and me in the basement, pitch-wise, and nothing in between. When she was done, she commanded "O Holy Night." Now she sounded like Chantal again. Then she circled back to Handel, now with her usual verve after the languid recitative opening.

As the last note wafted to the ceiling, Johnny spoke from the clinic door. "Chantal, could you bring Godzilla to the clinic so Mrs. Severn can see him? His name, by the way, is Sir Percy Nofurr."

Chantal wrinkled her nose in disgust. "No way it is."

"This is our last chance to practice, unless you want to hide out in my room with the electric keyboard. Do you want to go over anything again? Mrs. Severn can wait," I said.

"JD, I've been singing all of these pieces half my life. I can fake my way through one more time." She lifted Godzilla into her arms. He laid his head on her shoulder and raised a lip at me to show the dental weapons he'd used on Darryl.

Good for Chantal, restored to her big, bold self. I wondered where I was going to find the same confidence. I followed her at a distance, Godzilla with his baleful blue eyes on me. I didn't plan on any sudden moves.

Anelia Severn jumped to her feet when Chantal entered the examination room. She was bundled up to her chin and down to her wrists. The marks on her face were barely visible under expert makeup.

Godzilla broke into a wail longer than Chantal's high note in "O Holy Night," about the same pitch too. Chantal poured him into Anelia's arms, a liquid transfer. Tears spurted across her cheeks and dropped on his skin, making little dark pink splotches. I felt like I should leave them in such a private moment, but I didn't. Chantal would need support when Godzilla returned to his life as Sir Percy.

She stood right next to Anelia, where she could scratch the cat's head as she described his adventures over the last few days. He clung to Anelia, but he nuzzled Chantal's cheeks, also wet.

Passive as a Buddha, Johnny studied them as the women descended into baby talk, with Godzilla leaning toward one, then the other. It helped that Anelia was just a few inches taller than Chantal.

Anelia pulled her cat close for a hug. Chantal wiped her eyes as she fetched his blue satin carrier and set it on the examining table.

Anelia shook her head. "He just used that as a toy and a place to hide. It's never been able to hold him. You'll want a stronger one when he has to travel."

Chantal looked puzzled, and Johnny raised an eyebrow.

Anelia drew a deep breath. "The policeman said he'd wrap up Doug's death right away, that I could leave town whenever I want. Tomorrow I'm going back to Hungary, where I was born. My grandparents are still there, and my mother returned ten years ago. I would have gone earlier, but I didn't want to leave Percy. He's not a good traveler. He couldn't handle a nine-hour flight." The tears started again. "But if I'd been brave and found him a new home, Doug wouldn't have had the chance to be cruel to him, and—so many things would have been different, if I hadn't been such a coward."

She looked at me. "You said he'd be safe here. Can he stay? I'll contribute to his care. You'll find him a good home? It takes a special person to care for a Sphynx. They have different needs from other cats."

Chantal scooped him from her arms and snuggled him. His face stretched into bizarre expressions. "He's got a good home, the best home, with me. I know all about bathing him and oiling him, special diets, and special clothes. You should see the little jammies I made him. He tore them up this morning, though. I guess they're only for when it's freezing."

Anelia gave a watery laugh. "He must have been really cold. He's torn up so many sweaters. I bought him a little kitty heating pad and wrapped it in the remains of his sweaters. I'll bring it to you. And his cosmetics."

I said, "Chantal slept with him in a sleeping bag by the fire last night."

"Oh! I know you'll take good care of him then. Will your boyfriend love him too?"

We all exchanged glances at the fear shadowing her voice. Chantal assured her, "I won't be getting one of that endangered species unless Godzilla likes him. Lovers are everywhere, but a good cat is hard to find."

Johnny, who thinks all cats are good, nodded, satisfied.

Dianne entered the clinic behind me with Nevada in her arms. "Johnny, can I leave Nevada in here for a while? We're using my room as the women's dressing room, and she keeps escaping, which isn't good with all these people coming and going. The rest of our cats are in your bedroom. We're using JD's for the men's dressing room."

"Sure, feel free, and thanks for asking," I said. No one paid any attention.

Dianne pushed around me but stopped short when she saw Godzilla. He flattened his bat ears, and Nevada fluffed out.

Anelia dabbed at her eyes. "I'd better go, or I won't be able to, not without him. Percy, you be a good boy in your new home. I'll always love you, no matter how far away I am. If I ever come back—may I see him?"

"Of course," cried Chantal. "We can do FaceTime or Zoom if you want to visit from afar."

In the weepy leave-taking, Dianne murmured, "I guess we're getting a new cat."

I whispered back, "Chantal is."

Anelia ran out the clinic door without looking back.

Chantal swayed in her bliss, her arms around Godzilla on the examining table. He looked from Johnny to me, as though we were the only blots in his perfect life. When his eyes rested on Nevada, his skin wrinkled. I guess cats with fur do that too, but you don't see their skin rippling, like there was an alien underneath.

Chantal's glow dimmed, and she pressed her forehead to his wrinkly one. "Guys. I live in a rented room, and I'm hardly ever home. He'd be shut up for hours, days even when I travel. Probably scream the whole time. Could he stay here? And I'd be here more often, even pay rent?"

"Of course, both of you," said Johnny. He would have said the same for a tiger.

Silence hung in the air, getting heavier as the others took in Dianne's not-thrilled expression as she cuddled Nevada. Chantal avoided Dianne's eyes and looked at me. "JD?"

I folded my arms in a defensive stance. "I'm sure Johnny has a plan to rehabilitate Godzilla so that he doesn't shred every man he sees, but that kind of trust doesn't happen overnight. I'll agree to his staying here if Dianne does, because she's the one who'll be taking care of him when you're not here."

Dianne's uncertain expression turned to anguish. This was her best friend asking. Maybe I should have said No so she wouldn't be the refuser. In her internal battle, her grip on her own cat slackened. Nevada swirled her plumed fluffy tail and launched herself out of Dianne's arms. She landed on the examining table and locked her laser-blue eyes with Godzilla's, just a foot away. The humans in the room stopped breathing.

Then Nevada took a step forward and touched her nose to his, not friendly, just allowing his existence in her space. Godzilla flicked his whip of a tail once, to say that he could take on the whole house if he felt like it, but he just didn't, not at the moment. I foresaw a long happy life of their ignoring each other.

Dianne's face sank into a full-on, happiest of happy smiles. "I don't mind taking care of him, and I'd love to have you here more often."

"I'll give my landlady a month's notice right away," Chantal promised as she gathered her cat into her arms once more. He showed me his fangs again.

I gave him a finger wave, but not within reach of the death blades on his paws. "Welcome to the madhouse."

CHAPTER 22

In the sighs that filled the room, Johnny asked, "What are we wearing this evening?"

I braced myself to hear that we'd be wearing ABBA drag, satin suits in a rainbow of colors. But Chantal, still nuzzling Godzilla's forehead, mumbled, "You like being called 'Zil?' Or you wanna be 'God?' Oh, I know! How about 'Magnificat?' But how am I gonna shorten that?" She looked at me and cleared her throat to declare, "Dianne and I are wearing our Great Waltz formals. You guys ought to wear your tuxes."

I bet we're the only two guys ever who were relieved to hear that. We headed upstairs to start the process. Sophie Thi was applying makeup to a Cortez cousin, with someone I didn't recognize, no doubt a performer, waiting next in a line that extended across the couch and then snaked around the entertainment area.

Her client beautified, Sophie Thi sold her some eyeliner and then announced to the room, "I'm taking a break. Back in fifteen. You do the same."

She sat down on the stool she hadn't used and wiggled her toes as she guzzled from a nearby bottle of water. "I'm doing the performers too. You guys want to get in line for that?"

As the once and future clients milled around, chatting, Johnny fell back on the ropes of indecision. His eyebrows coming together a quarter inch told me he wanted to accept his sister's offer but would rather die than appear in public in makeup, unless—

"Wow, thanks!" I enthused. "That would be awesome for camera or stage, but I'm not sure about chamber music. The audience will be close enough to pluck our nose hairs, and we'd look like clowns in makeup. Are you doing the other male performers?" I injected my voice with some FOMO anxiety, to show I was afraid of missing out what the cool kids were doing.

"Other guys are performing? Haven't seen 'em. But let me know if you want something for stage or camera." She pulled out more palettes and brushes from her endless travel case, revealing stacks of small bills tucked in one of the lower drawers. She wore the same scoop-necked tunic she'd worn all weekend, now with matching woolly tights. Today she'd decorated the tunic with a spangly scarlet infinity scarf, multiple gauzy layers following the neckline with shiny doodads sticking up and out all over. Adding to the interesting 3D effect was an old-fashioned necklace, dripping with rubies, winking with diamonds, partially hidden by the scarf. Occasional blazes peeped out as she moved.

"Profitable trip?" I asked.

She gnawed her lip and then reapplied lipstick. "Yeah. Maybe I shouldn't be? Profiting off family, I mean? They've been really nice to me, the sisters and cousins."

"I doubt you've forced anything on them or that they bought more than they can afford," I soothed. My sisters, at least, were capable of showing their purchases to the fam while saying, "This is what I want for Christmas."

Her brow cleared. "I know. I'll give them each a lipstick. Good?"

Johnny and I agreed that lipstick was always appropriate, like we even knew.

"That's a nice necklace," Johnny commented.

I frowned, trying to remember whether he'd ever complimented anyone's appearance or apparel.

Sophie Thi pulled back the infinity scarf to reveal the necklace. "Some lady brought it over today. She looked like she'd been through the wars, so I did her makeup for her. Good thing I practiced on your sisters. She was a blonde. Granny Deb said I could wear the necklace tonight. I thought I'd better just keep it around my neck. I don't want to lose it. Granny Deb said it's been in the family a long time. Thought she was gonna cry."

"Yes. I think there's some diamond bracelets too. And a ring?" Johnny asked.

"Yeah, Granny Deb's wearing those. Maybe they were being cleaned, I don't know."

"Something like that, I'm sure," Johnny agreed. "I'm glad you're taking good care of it."

I put my hand on his elbow and steered him to my room, claiming I needed his advice on my tux. That raised his eyebrows. No one ever asked his advice on clothes.

I didn't either. Shutting the door, I asked, "Did you agree with the suicide verdict for Dianne's sake—or mine, Mrs. Severn's, Sophie Thi's, your grandmother's, Godzilla's, or someone else's?"

In the following silence—after a year, it still amazes me how sound-proof the house is— he pushed aside clothes in the closet to get to my tux. "I didn't want to explain a bullet from Dianne's gun in the brick work, though she didn't shoot him, but I wasn't aware of any divided loyalties. Justice has been done, as much justice as there is in life. Doug Severn will no longer abuse anyone. They are free to begin new lives—Godzilla, Anelia Severn, even Sophie Thi. My grandmother has her heirlooms again. Neither you nor Dianne will be brought into a murder investigation."

Icicles on the eaves gave up the ghost with a snap and crashed to the ground below. We both jumped.

I asked, "Do you think Anelia Severn killed her husband? She loved her cat enough to give him up, and she gave back the jewelry her husband stole, but that doesn't mean she didn't shoot him and make it look like a suicide."

"You spent more time talking to her than I did. You probably have a better idea than I do. If so, it could only be called self-defense." Johnny pretended to examine my tux like he cared, as though I hadn't sent it to the cleaners the last time I wore it (the Great Waltz at the University of Texas in October).

I moved to my bed, where someone had returned the previous night's sheets and blankets. I threw aside the borrowed pillowcase and top sheet, redolent of the gardenia perfume the Cortez women love, for the laundry, though I admit I did it slowly. The replacements I pulled out from the closet, across from my tux, didn't smell nearly as wonderful. "Circumstances can push people to do anything, the nicest people, the hateful ones, the ones who never thought about it. Prisons aren't full of the most evil people in the world. I agree that self-defense would be easy to establish here. Anelia Severn bears marks of abuse."

"As does her cat, even if they're not on the outside." Johnny shrugged one shoulder and then picked up the opposite side of the top sheet to tuck it in. "I can't speculate in the absence of forensic data, and there won't be any, since the death has been accepted as a suicide."

I didn't look at him as I folded a corner of the top sheet and shoved it under the mattress. "And you didn't see anything to contradict that. Did you look?" We moved on to the blanket and comforter.

Johnny smoothed out wrinkles and said, "I looked as much as any reasonable person would have."

I snorted. Johnny thinks that bar's flat on the ground.

He walked to the window and gazed out over the porch and front lawn, both soggy with melting ice and snow. We measure Texas winter in individual days, not months. "I was sure that as justice of the peace I'd always pursue the truth, no matter where it took me. I've always believed that dealing with the truth has to be better than dealing with lies."

"Something change your mind?" I kept smoothing the comforter, pretending there were wrinkles. The soft polished cotton was soothing.

"I'm not sure. But for the first time, I could see no advantage to anyone being prosecuted for a murder. Doug's dead; it can't matter to him. He killed the only friends we knew of and abused those he lived with. Qui bono? I couldn't think of anyone who would benefit from an investigation."

"Your conscience is happy with that?" I asked, having much experience with Johnny's inconvenient conscience.

"I'll discuss it with my rabbi and my teacher at the sangha."

"If they disagree with your inaction, you'll reopen the case?" I blanched at the thought.

"No, but I'll take their wisdom into account on future cases."

There were other points I could make, like what about society, but I was sure his rabbi and Buddhism teacher would cover those.

CHAPTER 23

Chantal texted me that the cellist was ready to rehearse and we could have fifteen minutes at the piano if I would hustle my butt downstairs. I did, grabbing presents to stuff under the tree on my way.

Because Chantal and the cellist had already discussed the piece, we barely needed the fifteen minutes. Like every young professional musician, they had performed "Rejoice Greatly" every Christmas for a decade. I hadn't, not every year, but I tried not to get in their way.

I wondered what I was doing here, an amateur among professionals. The delicious aromas from the kitchen and the food tables smelled like garbage to me. I grabbed the nearest something wrapped in bread and gulped it down with a glass of water. If I sat at the dinner table, I'd have to meet all these musicians and hear résumés that would put me to shame. "Lessons with my grandmother and singing in a band" didn't sound like much next to Juilliard, the Met, the Tchaikovsky Competition, and so on into the heights.

I joined the greeters at the front door, even with Chantal calling that I didn't have to. I needed something to contain the terror of the worst imposter syndrome I'd ever known, that I had the nerve to do something I called making music in the company of people who actually could.

The first people to arrive—again—were the Brandons, minus Melanie. Miss Leigh was a concert sponsor, but no one expected her to show up after a death in the family.

Clutching her friend Debbie Ly's hand, Miss Leigh, draped in sober black, murmured, "I just had to get out and think about something else. Melanie's asleep."

Claire, also darkly clad, sought out Johnny on his way from the kitchen. She pressed a festive box the size of a phone into his hands. "You'll want to put this away. It's the good stuff. I'm sorry there's not more. Melanie ate half of them. That's why she's passed out."

Murmuring thanks, Johnny selected one chocolate the size of a dime to melt in his mouth. That was just for politeness; the concert would be over before it kicked in. I reminded myself of that to keep my hands out of the box. I cast a longing glance at the globe-shaped liquor cabinet, but that would have to wait until I'd humiliated myself. A glass of any alcohol before a performance would destroy whatever skill I have. I've tested that theory.

Johnny asked Darryl to take any children who didn't care to hear the concert to join the security team in the cat shelter to serve, protect, and play video games. The Quiston boys thundered toward the back door before Johnny finished his sentence, giving Darryl the chance to mutter as he gestured towards the gift box. "I guess you have to be polite, but she must use oregano. I didn't feel anything at all."

Harmony, echoed by her younger cousin Mary, announced in their most grownup voices that they'd attend the concert. They then dashed to join their new best friends, the Cortez women, in a gigglefest on the back row.

With all the sponsors and half of the elves on duty at the door, I had no excuse for being there. I could hear the real performers warming up upstairs, so I went into the clinic to do my own vocal exercises, more for something to do than with any expectation of improvement. The resident cats looked alarmed, and Godzilla joined me in vocal gymnastics. He sounded better than I did.

At one minute before start time, I rejoined the world. The sponsors and people who deserved it—donors, maybe?—sat in the front row of a full hall. I spotted Mrs. Ly, Miss Leigh, and Claire. Beside her, their shoulders touching, was Pastor Nathan. That gave me a flicker of happiness, but I felt even more nauseous when I saw how many more chairs had been added to the side and back. Even the sponsors hadn't expected a full house, much less a fuller-than-full house. At first I told myself they were for the local church choirs who would sing the final number, but that was just self-deception: the rows of chairs for the performers, extending from the dining area into the kitchen, were just as full.

On my way to that dungeon, I passed my grandmother. She was saying to the guest next to her, "My grandson is performing tonight."

Her voice, swollen with pride as big as a Hill Country peach, answered why I was doing this. I comforted myself with the thought that at least I wasn't making an idiot of myself in court. Then I saw a local judge and some attorneys in the audience. That's the horrible thing about chamber music: you can actually see the horde of rabid critics disguised as friends and relatives. But Grandmother would still be proud, though too much of a musician not to know the difference between me and the real musicians.

I stumbled over to the performers' pen, where Dianne gestured to the chair next to her. She and Chantal, on her other side, grinned and held up their presents from me, Merry as the Virgin Mary with Godzilla the Demon Child crawling all over her and Chantal looking like some tender saint gazing at the Demon Child cuddling in her lap. Of course, they'd found their presents under the tree. I should have put the gifts in a safe deposit box if I didn't want them opened early.

"My mother decided they were St. Gertrude, the early years, and St. Julian of Norwich, or maybe St. Clare," whispered Dianne.

I sighed in relief. I hadn't wanted Mrs. Cortez to think I was blaspheming the Virgin Mary. "Cat-associated saints, I presume?"

Dianne nodded.

"You scared?" I asked as I took the chair she saved for me. Lingering dinner aromas in the kitchen made me sorry I'd skipped the meal.

She shrugged. "I'm not doing anything I haven't done for years—Christmas carols and ABBA songs."

"Oh. I'm playing Handel too."

"You've played it every day since the first of November, and you learned it in college, when Chantal wanted you to practice with her every day, because she was allowed only so many sessions with her real accompanist."

I quit seeking comfort and just contemplated my doom. Dianne surprised me by giving my hand a quick squeeze, more of a spasm, but I appreciated the effort. It didn't carry me through, because we were the next-to-last act. Singers, a brass quintet, string trio, guitar quartet, flautist, and a couple of pianists preceded us.

Finally it was Chantal's turn. I took my place at the piano and stalled by fiddling with the bench height. To my surprise, Johnny took the page turner's chair beside me. To avoid being included in the band's choreography, he always made sure he had another job, either playing bass guitar or turning pages, even though I'd memorized everything long ago. I was grateful for the support.

Chantal was in great voice, the cellist provided a solid foundation for her, and I didn't wreck anything.

Then MultiABBA assembled (with Johnny turning pages), and we broke into the same holiday tunes we sang at the previous party, adding some with classical roots in acknowledgement of our upgraded venue. To my surprise, I was having fun. As we again belted out "Happy New Year," I realized what we do better than anybody, training or no training. Our voices blend together perfectly into one sweet whole. Sure, the piano and our vocal cords vibrated, but this blending was a whole-body experience, like another being created from our four voices. As my tingling fingers caressed the smooth keys, I saw a similar joy in my friends' faces—our audience's too, like we were giving them a gift to be allowed in our swirling harmonies.

I took a deep breath to bellow one last "Happy New Year," and inhaled that forever-familiar MultiABBA-Black Orchid aroma: sweat mixed with Dianne's gardenia perfume, Chantal's citrusy scent from her favorite East Texas parfumier, the eleventy herbs and spices from whatever Johnny was cooking. I took an extra sniff; it was marvelous.

After we bowed into the applause, Dianne and Chantal stepped behind me to close ranks. As Dianne pushed Johnny's shoulder to make him sit down again, she said in her quietest voice as I strummed the opening chords, "Special request. You don't know this one."

In contrast with ABBA's wall of sound, cranked to eleven, "Ahavat Olam" opened in a whisper, barely a vibration from the instrument or the voices, like the lullaby Chantal called it.

Dianne was wrong. Johnny did know that prayer-song, and so did others in the audience. Mrs. Ly, the slim, bearded man next to her—Johnny's rabbi, I remembered—and several musicians joined Johnny in expressions of dawning wonder. Some, like him, mouthed the Hebrew words silently.

It was a short song, but it gave us so many harmonic opportunities: me providing a bass cushion for the soaring women's voices, right up to the ceiling; tossing the melody between us like a tennis volley; weaving and chasing each other in counterpoint, all the while increasing the volume to the English language bridge, with heavenly assurances everybody could understand.

Darryl peeked into the room from the cat clinic at that point, as our voices swelled loud enough to carry to the cats, still in our ABBA-voice-meld. The joy on his face flipped into horror as he mouthed some words not part of the prayer.

Two cats, one shimmering pale gold, the other hairless pink, trotted across the stage area to seek their people. Not missing a beat or a note, Dianne and Chantal intercepted them before tragedy could strike. The women cradled their feline friends as they crooned the song's return to its quiet beginnings, singing the lullaby to their beloveds. Johnny at least appreciated their serenading the feline part of creation.

As I nudged the keys for the last time, he whispered, "And let the people say—"

"Meooooow!" yowled Nevada (alto) and Godzilla (bass).

The audience burst into applause as thunderous as yesterday's storm on the roof.

The women popped quick bows before running into the clinic with their distressed friends. It felt wrong to accept all the acclaim for myself, so I extended an arm in their direction as I stood and nodded my head in acknowledgement.

Despite the din I could hear Mrs. Ly on the first row, she who abandoned her religion on the battlefields in Vietnam, say to the rabbi in tender, teary accents, "My mother used to whisper Ahavat Olam to me every night."

The applause swelled again with the women's catless return, which made Chantal think we needed an encore. She picked a rousing Hanukkah song, which was fine with me. I could have sung "Ninety-nine Bottles of Beer on the Wall" with just as much verve and gusto. I was thrilled to be making music with my forever friends. Even with screeching cats, weird parties, smells and tastes of food from worldwide cultures, and even police investigations, there was no place I'd rather be. During our last ovation, I threw my arms around all of them until they squawked while the choirs pushed their way on stage for the big choral finish.

Chantal, she who has "Let's have a party/put on a show" tattooed on her genes, knew the best way to get an audience was to put them in the show, so she'd invited all the local church choirs to sing excerpts from Bach's "Magnificat." We clustered close together, mingling the Black Orchids scents with more perfume and sweat, and hollered "Magnificat!" at the top of our lungs, shaking the rafters and vibrating every surface and dental filling.

I felt sorry for the people watching football in their homes. Nothing could top this.

SONGS FROM
MULTIABBA'S HOLIDAY PLAYLIST

If you enjoyed this book, won't you leave a review at your favorite bookseller's site? For giveaways and news, sign up for my newsletter at my website.

https://dimond.me

I've talked the characters into blogging there, and I'm working on getting them to do the newsletter too.

If you're curious about the songs MultiABBA sang, you can hear the whole list on Spotify or single tracks on YouTube.

https://open.spotify.com/playlist/4pWaKKxDzUasnWlbUO0F4s?si=
da5349ea1143444d

Ode to Freedom (ABBA) https://youtu.be/YtNJybve8j4
Pachelbel's Tantrum (The Therapy Sisters)
https://youtu.be/YCIDMnASngU

Christmas in Texas (The Studebakers) *Bonus track not on playlist*! https://youtu.be/iv5GQe6Mo6k

Mi Burrito Sabanero (Juana) https://youtu.be/lJawRaON8h0

Ven a Cantar (Grupo Hanyak) https://youtu.be/5PLKGM9t0fc

This Joy (Resistance Revival Chorus) https://youtu.be/1TbDPwA09Bc

Makom Bina (Deborah Sacks Mintz with the Hadar Ensemble) https://youtu.be/RorTgwYagt4

Ma-oz Tzur (featuring Dana Kirstein, Erran Baron Cohen) https://youtu.be/R8J22yFFNdg

Carol of the Bells (Pentatonix) https://youtu.be/WSUFzC6_fp8

Holly and the Ivy (Mediaeval Baebes) https://youtu.be/57l6dSbVppM

Lo, How a Rose E'er Blooming (Robert Shaw, Robert Shaw Chamber Singers) https://youtu.be/SVpJrf_clgo

Joy to the World (Celtic Women) https://youtu.be/VDmIddF7DfQ

Happy New Year (ABBA) https://youtu.be/3Uo0JAUWijM

Rejoice Greatly from Handel's *Messiah* (Jeanine De Bique with Chineke!) https://youtu.be/bHQpeGzio4k Spotify list has different artist.

Ahavat Olam (Platt Brothers) https://youtu.be/1yhk_obX7CQ

Hanerot Halalu by Rabbi Miriam Margles (Rebezra) https://youtu.be/Y--HPIpJSuQ

Movement 1 from Bach's Magnificat BVW 243 (Ricercar Consort) https://youtu.be/y-k_ec_BPMc

SNEAK PEAK FROM FAMILY MATTERS

I was lazing through an August morning, hearing only office sounds: the four Very Good Kitties scrabbling down the dark wooden hall floor, my partner Dianne (CPA, CFE) doing syncopated samba steps on the way to her office, a cat yowling in fury or pain in my other partner Johnny's vet clinic, and at our reception desk, our intern Darryl practicing the soprano part to "Dancing Queen" in Spanish. Just your normal detective's office in disguise as a law, accountancy, and veterinary firm—and an ABBA tribute band.

When the phone rang, Darryl said in a completely different voice, "Black Orchid Enterprises. Law offices of James Daniel Thompson. May I help you? Just a moment. I'll see if Mr. Thompson is available."

He tiptoed into my office, in one of Gregg House's two turrets, and mouthed, "JD, it's your father."

I made a gagging face and picked up the phone. "Hi, Dad. Got just a few minutes between clients—" If you define "a few" as those spanning 9:30 a.m. to 2:00 p.m.

"I won't keep you," he snapped. "When's the last time you heard from Merry?"

I frowned, thinking. At age twenty, my twin sisters Merry and Cherry were entering their last year of college. Keeping in touch with their brother wasn't high on their To-Do list. "Not sure. I usually see them when I visit the grandparents in Waco, when we get everybody together for a meal. But Merry went to Dallas for the summer, and—"

"I'm not sure she did. I tried to call her when I was in Dallas last week. I stopped by the place she said she worked too."

Idly I wondered if he'd ever let me finish a thought or a sentence. I remembered Merry's social media post about getting a job at Doo-Wop Burger, one of those trying-to-be-vintage diner chains. She wore their terminally cute uniform and posed with a silly grin in front of their icon, a huge dancing cheeseburger.

She and her sister had a lifelong experience of cute. Mother adored her blonde, curly-haired, blue-eyed twins. After inflicting old-fashioned family names on them (Meredith Arline and Charity Adrienne), she gave them the unsuitable nicknames of Merry and Cherry. Merry is thoughtful, and Cherry isn't generous. Mother dressed them in pastels with maximum ribbons, ruffles, and bows from the day they were born, shortly before my ninth birthday, with the result that they looked like frilly potatoes, despite being skinny as pencils. (I admit I was underwhelmed to receive two baby sisters instead of a PlayStation. And even with just a vague concept of where babies came from, I was nauseated.) I spent my teen years babysitting them, which didn't improve our relationship. After our mother died of cancer when they were eleven and I was nineteen, I made a point to go home more, the better to be miserable together. I also brought them to visit me at college. Hanging out with my female housemates filled them with pride. I thought when they got to college we might have adult friendships, but they hadn't much use for an older brother unless they needed help moving.

Dad growled, "Your grandparents haven't seen her recently. She came here a few times in June and July, always wanting money. Not that Cherry hasn't done the same all summer. But Merry never said she'd left that job, and she never sent me her Dallas address."

I actually heard a sliver of worry in his voice. Touching, it was. "I'll check with Dianne. They both still stay in touch with her. Cherry doesn't know anything either?"

"She says not. She says she and Merry have been trying to live their own lives instead of being practically Siamese twins. This summer was going to be the big split, with Merry going to Dallas to pursue some guy." The disapproval faucet was on full blast.

I remembered Merry's Instagram photo with the caption "Going to Dallas to be near my darling J!"

My father called me back to the present with a cough. "They've exchanged texts over the summer, nothing that alarmed Cherry. She's sure Merry will show up for school in a few weeks."

"I'm sure she's right," I agreed, based on nothing at all. "I'll ask around and get back to you. Good-bye and have a nice day to you too," I said to the dial tone.

Just then a note from Darryl popped up on our office channel that proved he could work and sing at the same time: his suggestions for the next week's social media. I can't see the point in advertising our services to the world when we're geographically confined to Central Texas, just south of Austin, but I'm told you never turn down free advertising.

For Throwback Thursday, Darryl proposed a Thompson family Easter photo from around fifteen years ago: Me at thirteen, forcing the corners of my mouth up despite clenched teeth, my hands clawing the shoulders of two wiggly twins, already sugared up on their Easter candy breakfast, their ruffly blue spring dresses matching their skin, because Texas always turns arctic for Easter just to show that it can. I could still hear the preceding conversation: "Adrienne, we're going to be late for church." "I still don't have a good picture of them in their dresses. JD, would you hold them still?" That was the twins' cue to ramp it up to eleven. It was an Easter miracle that we were all in focus. I've always known the answer to the Biblical question "Am I my sisters' keeper?" the answer being "Hell, yes."

I hesitated to approve the photo but couldn't think of a reason to object. We already had Dianne at age five, dancing the Macarena at one of her mother's parties, and eight-year-old Johnny helping in his grandfather's Vietnamese restaurant in downtown Beauchamp. It was my turn, and if I turned down this one, the next suggestion would be worse, maybe the last Easter photo before Mother died, because we all knew it was coming, with the twins grinning like maniacs over their holiday ruffles and me not any better. Nobody smiled in the next year's photo, with Cherry as Goth as a twelve-year-old is allowed to be, Merry in a colorless straight shift, her hair bobbed into a straight line that echoed her compressed lips, and me looking like I had a toothache but still auditioning for Future Lawyers of America. Dad didn't bother with Easter photos after that.

I walked across the hall, wide enough to be a room in its own right, to the other turret office. Darryl had moved on to "Chiquitita." I sang a few notes of my bass-baritone part, just for encouragement. Darryl has a nice falsetto and is working on substituting for our soprano in our ABBA tribute band. Since finishing school, we don't perform much as we used to, but Dianne's mother is an event planner, and she occasionally lands us quinceañeras and other Latinx gigs.

Dianne herself was gazing at her computer screen with a rapt expression that meant (1) she was in love or (2) she'd just created the most awesome spreadsheet ever. I was going with the latter. Her deep, happy sigh meant that she'd beat the numbers into submission yet again. Her golden, blue-eyed kitten Nevada slept on the desk, in easy petting range.

Dianne is easily the most gorgeous woman I've ever seen, even though she's my three-time ex: almost six feet of warm brown skin and blacker-than-black hair shining around her shoulders. As I fiddled with my phone, I asked, "Dianne, have you heard from Merry?"

"No, I heard from Cherry recently though." Being Dianne, she then proceeded to check her answer by scrolling through past texts. She frowned. "I'm wrong. Merry texted me about three weeks ago. Nothing much, just checking in. But Cherry did text me a few days before that, asking whether I thought she should change her name to Cheryl or Cherie or something. She's worried that no one will take her seriously as Cherry, except maybe in adult films. I must have been thinking of that."

My sisters met Dianne when they were ten, when I brought Dianne home for some holiday as The Girlfriend(TM). After we broke up for the first time less than a year later, they sobbed, "But you don't have to break up with *us*." Dianne agreed, and took them under her wing because, as she said, "What's two more hermanas y primas?"

Dianne's the eldest of five siblings and many, many cousins. Though she'll tell you in the first ten minutes on your first date that she's never having children, for more than ten years she's taken all the sisters and cousins at least twice a year to pick out clothes. Her mother and aunts are confident that she'll choose things for modest Catholic girls, and the girls are sure that she's going to make all their fantasies of style and allure come true. It's a testament to Dianne's skills that all parties always think they got what they wanted.

Merry and Cherry were thrilled to join the Cortez pilgrimages to the Hillsboro discount mall. A few years after our mother died, Grandmother made the ceremonial trip to Merle Norman so they could learn about makeup, but, not laboring under the same delusions as the Cortez mothers, she was thrilled to have Dianne's help with fashionable clothes and later, a trip to Planned Parenthood for all the essentials of young womanhood. Merry and Cherry made fast friends with Dianne's sisters closest to their own ages, Tima and Juke. The Cortez brother Zap, two years older, grew more admiring as the twins grew up.

Guadalupe Dianne Cortez and her siblings are a testament to their mother's devotion to the Virgin Mary. Instead of naming them all "María," Conchita Cortez chose Marian shrines for their names, with a backup Anglo name for emergencies. Dianne moved to her middle name in college after a lifetime of schoolyard teasing about "Lupita." So I could see why Cherry would turn to her for advice. Our mother loved that nickname, but there are limits to what you can do for your dead mother. Cherry works it as best she can, often wearing or dying her hair cherry and collecting cherry blossom jewelry and fascinators.

My phone squawked. I shrugged at the results. "Merry's got autorespond on for texts, probably voice too. 'Can't answer my phone at work. Back atcha later.'"

"Problem?" asked Dianne as she stroked Nevada's forehead.

I leaned against the dark wood door jamb. "My father's worried about my sister Merry. He visited the place she was supposed to be working in

Dallas and found she hadn't been in for months. So he—and I—are looking for people who've heard from her recently."

Dianne's eyebrows raised in wonder. She said in a hushed voice, "Wow. Your father called you for help." She focused on her screens and typed a bit before saying, "I blasted all my sisters and cousins, asking for the last time anyone heard from her. Merry and Cherry are on the Hermanas y Primas list, too; maybe they'll realize people are worried."

Footsteps in the hall announced the approach of Dr. John Ky Ly (DVM), our other partner, after his morning vet appointments. "JD, would you come with me on a justice of the peace call? We can bring back lunch."

I jumped, conflating his actions with my own worries. As Assistant Justice of the Peace, Johnny had to examine every dead body in Alvarez County. But Merry lived in Waco. She couldn't be the dead body he was going to see. Definitely probably not.

ABOUT THE AUTHOR

After stints in professional orchestras, law firms, cat rescue, bookkeeping, and technical communication, M. R. Dimond returned to a childhood dream of writing fiction, which has turned out to be about musicians, lawyers, veterinarians, accountants, and cats. Watch for the next Black Orchid Enterprises mystery in early 2023.

Also by M. R. Dimond

Birth of the Black Orchids
"Blessed" in *Dreaming the Goddess*, Karen Dales, editor
"Nine Lives Through Time" in *Cat Tales, War Zone*, Rebecca McFarland Kyle and Dana Bell, editors
"Carol for Mixed Voices" in *Best of Strange Horizons Year 2*

Acknowledgements

My page count reminds me to conclude, but I cannot leave without thanking family, friends, teachers, my fantastic artistic community, and all the cats, so many cats, for all the love and support. A million kisses to all of you!